Flying Over Water

Flying Over Water

By **SHANNON HITCHCOCK**
and **N. H. SENZAI**

SCHOLASTIC PRESS / NEW YORK

Library of Congress Cataloging-in-Publication Data available

ISBN 978-1-338-61766-5

10 9 8 7 6 5 4 3 2 1   20 21 22 23 24

Printed in the U.S.A.   23
First edition, October 2020

Book design by Abby Dening

For Beth and Cheyenne, who first piqued my
interest in Islam.

—SWH

For those who build bridges, not walls.

—NHS

CHAPTER ONE

☙ NOURA ❧

Monday, January 30, 2017

own . . . down . . . down . . . Nearly forty thousand feet down . . . With a gulp, I turned away from the plane's small oval window and yanked down the shade. We were way, *way* up there; traveling in a metal tube, with no net to catch us if we plummeted to the ground.

"Are you all right, *habibti?*" whispered a comforting voice.

"Yes, Baba," I whispered back, careful not to wake my twin brother, Ammar, who sat between us. His handsome face was smooth and carefree in sleep, instead of creased in its usual frown.

"It's exciting, eh?" Baba grinned. "This whole flying thing?"

I shrugged, my mind buzzing with a thousand thoughts and emotions that fought with each other to be heard. *Happiness. Fear. Wonder. Grief.* Usually I would have shared them all, talkative as a magpie, but not today. Not on the first ever airplane ride of my life, where all the sights and sensations made me feel like I was drowning.

"It'll be okay, my love," he said. "We're here together, safe."

I nodded, muffling a yawn as I looked into his reassuring soft gray eyes, where hope and comfort lay intertwined. It was true; it was a miracle that we were here. *Together. Safe.* Across the aisle sat Mama, her lips moving silently as her fingers worried a strand of amber prayer beads. Ismail sat curled beside her, sucking his thumb and watching cartoons. The personal television screens were one of a dozen things that had fascinated me the moment we'd boarded. Who knew the seats would be so cushiony, that you got your own tiny table and that the flight attendants gave you all the orange soda you wanted to drink? And they'd brought warm socks for my feet, eye masks for sleeping (though I hadn't slept even a moment in all the excitement), coloring books and pencils, and hot food in little trays covered in foil. They'd even brought small paper cups of ice cream, my favorite, for dessert!

I stretched, my muscles stiff from six hours of sitting, and propped my head against the tiny pillow. This was the second plane I'd been on; the first, a giant German Airbus, had plucked us from Istanbul Airport and headed west to

Frankfurt. Arriving late, we'd disembarked and hurried through the warren-like halls of the airport. My lavender hijab fluttered behind me until we arrived, breathless, for our connecting flight. As we'd waited to board, Baba had cradled Mama's shoulder, both of them staring out the window as tears flowed down her cheeks. Mama's brother, two sisters, and mother had fled Syria four years prior and found asylum in Berlin, just an hour's flight away. I knew Mama had prayed we'd also end up in Germany, but fate was taking us elsewhere. *Without the chance of visiting our family even once.*

"Noura, wake up," urged a voice beside me. I sat up, disoriented. "What is it?"

"We're landing," Ammar said, with a rare smile. His upturned lips caused the wicked red scar that ran along the right side of his face to pucker.

As the plane's wheels descended, a grating sound rumbled beneath our seats. Ammar reached across me and lifted the window shade with a snap. I pressed my face against the cold glass and could practically feel the wispy clouds caress my cheek as we flew across the glowing blue sky. Startled, I glimpsed a large bird gliding beside us, its pink feathers glinting in the sun. A bright yellow eye peered at me from an intelligent face, its beak long and shaped like a spoon. A memory tickled my mind, of feeding the caged singing birds in Baba's hotel in Aleppo. Was this what it felt like to be a bird? To escape your cage and have the freedom to travel anywhere, at any time your heart desired?

I looked down, watching the line of blue sky meet the ground. But it wasn't ground I spied. It was inky blue, swirling cerulean, aquamarine and navy . . . *water*. We were flying over water . . . so much water. I dug my fingers into the armrests, startled by the sight. *Focus, Noura*, whispered Dr. Barakat's voice inside my head. I placed my right hand on my stomach and the left on my chest. Slowly, I breathed in through my nose, filling up my lower lungs with air. Then I exhaled, releasing all the air from my mouth.

"What's wrong?" asked Ammar. He leaned over and saw Tampa Bay beneath us. "Water . . ." he said as realization dawned on his worried face. "Do you need to switch seats?"

I shook my head, focused on my breathing. I remembered the beautiful pink bird and let go of the fear. I was flying. Flying over water, and over the terrible memories. *In control. Safe.*

"I'm okay," I said a minute later. "Really."

"Good," said Ammar, the relief in his voice smoothing away his frown.

"What happened?" Baba asked, putting down a magazine he'd been engrossed in.

"Nothing," I said with a smile. "We're about to land."

"Yes," Baba said, fastening his seat belt. "We have arrived."

The gruff-voiced immigration officer handed back our passports with an encouraging smile. "Mr. Yusuf Alwan, Mrs. Muna Alwan, Ammar Alwan, Noura Alwan, and Ismail Alwan, welcome to America."

"Thank you, sir," Baba said, his voice rough from over two hours of interviews and going over the thick stack of immigration documents. "Thank you so much."

And with those words, I realized that we'd officially been welcomed to America. *The United States. Florida. Tampa.* Words that had floated around in my head and formed strange sounds in my mouth the moment I'd heard them four months ago. I'd been sitting next to the window in Ms. Pamuk's class when I'd seen Baba race past, waving an envelope in the air, sending up puffs of dust with every pounding footstep till he'd disappeared around the corner.

I hadn't paid attention during the rest of class, instead counting the minutes till Ammar and I could run home to our family's container, identical to the thousands of others, in Kilis, the Turkish refugee camp. We'd found our parents sitting against the cushions in the front room, lost in thought.

What happened? I'd burst out, while Ammar stood, silent as usual, stoically by. Baba jumped up, as if he still couldn't believe it himself, to tell us we'd been granted asylum. *In America.* He and Ammar had joyfully hugged while Mama tried to smile, disappointment lurking at the corners of her mouth. I realized that she'd hoped we'd be going to Germany. Wondering whether to be happy or sad, I'd crawled into her lap, wishing the letter had brought her only joy.

Past the immigration booths, I followed Baba toward baggage claim, but I knew no suitcases waited for us. We'd arrived carrying the small handbags that held all the possessions we had in the world: a few pairs of clothes and the mementos we'd been able to snatch before leaving Aleppo. Gone were Mama's collection of poetry books, Baba's fancy suits that he wore to work, Ammar's art supplies, and my collection of bird figurines and trinkets. Except for one, a delicate peacock brooch hidden in my pocket.

"What do we do now?" asked Mama, exhaustion lining her pale, delicate face.

"They told us to go to the receiving area after immigration.

Someone is supposed to meet us there," said Baba with a hopeful smile.

We followed the other passengers out a set of double doors into a wide hall where dozens of people stood, waiting to collect relatives or friends. I skimmed the sea of faces, not wanting to make direct eye contact with anyone.

"There," said Ammar, grabbing Baba's arm. He pointed toward a sign in the distance, bobbing up and down.

It read, WELCOME, ALWAN FAMILY. A stocky man with a shock of white hair held the sign, a warm smile lighting his tanned, leathery face. He was with a small group of people, one a tall, willowy woman wearing a long skirt, jean jacket, and turquoise hijab. When we stopped in front of them, they stood for a moment, looking at each other uncertainly.

"*Salaam Alaikum,*" exclaimed the woman in hijab. "Are you Yusuf Alwan?"

"*Walaikum Salaam,*" said Baba. "Yes, I am him."

"Welcome," said the woman in Arabic, her hazel eyes warm. "My name is Amani Sofian. I'm here to help translate if you need it."

"*Shukran*, thank you," said Baba. "My older children and I speak English fairly well, but my wife and youngest son are still learning."

Amani smiled and reached for Mama's hand as the others crowded around. I inched away, feeling unsettled. Near the exit doors, I could hear a low rumbling noise, like engines revving.

"Hello," said the stocky man, turning to me with a grin. "You're Noura, right?"

I gave him a shaky nod.

"My name is Bob, Bob Sanchez. I'm here to take you to your new home. How was your flight?"

I swallowed, my throat suddenly dry as I tried to dredge up the English words from school and the shows we'd watched on the internet. "Hello, Mr. Bob. It was . . . good. Thank you."

"Let's get going," said Amani, exchanging a worried look with Bob. "We have a short drive, but there's been . . . a bit of trouble."

"Trouble?" said Baba, a look of concern crossing his face. "What kind of trouble?"

"Nothing that directly affects you," Bob said. "We can talk more about it once we get you settled in your apartment."

Baba nodded and we turned to follow Amani toward the exit. As we reached the doors, the rumble of engines increased. But it wasn't cars I saw, it was a crowd of people standing outside. The noise was coming from them . . . shouting, yelling, and chanting.

What's going on? I thought, inching closer to Ammar as we slipped through the doors. Dozens of people congregated outside, chanting and carrying signs I couldn't understand. One read, KEEP YOUR ORANGE HANDS OFF OUR CONSTITUTION! and another, NO BAN, NO WALL.

"Baba, what is happening?" I asked.

Before he could answer me, a harried young man in a dark suit pressed his business card into Amani's hand. "I'm a lawyer. Did they have trouble getting through immigration?"

"No." She shook her head. "They were lucky."

"Call us if there are problems," he said. "Lots of refugees are stranded in airports all across the country."

"Why would we have problems?" I asked Ammar, feeling my stomach churn.

"They don't want us here," he growled.

Don't want us here? But we'd traveled thousands of miles to be here. If they didn't want us, where would we go? Back home? Memories clashed in my mind . . . of buildings reduced to rubble, the boom of explosions, wailing sirens, children crying. *We can't go back there!* A sharp pain snapped me back from the past as I pinched the soft skin near my wrist.

A girl with bright blue hair approached with a smile, carrying a yellow sign: IMMIGRANTS MAKE AMERICA GREAT! The boy beside her carried another one: WE ARE ALL MUSLIMS NOW.

I rubbed away the lingering sting and grabbed Baba's hand. *What was going on?*

CHAPTER TWO

◈ JORDYN ◈

Monday, January 30, 2017

I fluffed the pillow on the twin bed that would belong to Noura Alwan, assuming her family was allowed into the United States. The Muslim travel ban had created a lot of confusion. We'd followed the news all weekend, afraid the Alwans would be sent back to Turkey.

"Try not to worry," Mom said. She tucked a strand of straight blond hair behind her ears. "With a little bit of luck, they should be able to get through."

I couldn't help but worry, though. I'd been moody and anxious for weeks, ever since the best day of my life had been totally ruined.

Mom moved through the tiny apartment, straightening cushions, arranging fresh flowers, and polishing off the bathroom mirror. When our church had donated furniture for the refugees, Mom had volunteered to make sure the apartment was homey and ready for their arrival.

Volunteering to help was like something *old Mom* would have done. *New Mom* had barely left our condo since she'd been released from the hospital. Until today. I crossed my fingers that this was a positive sign.

"Mr. Alwan managed an award-winning hotel in Aleppo," Mom said. "I'm sure this apartment will be a big step down for them." She sighed. "But I'll bet it's much nicer than living in a Turkish refugee camp."

My chest tightened as images flashed through my mind from the documentary we'd watched at church: apartments with gaping holes, mothers clutching their children, schools and hospitals smashed to rubble. I tried to imagine what it must be like to turn on the faucet and for no water to pour out, to sit in the dark and read by candlelight. To be unable to watch television, or too afraid to play outside.

After viewing the film, Reverend Dixon had quoted Leviticus 19:33–34:

"When an alien resides with you in your land, you shall not oppress the alien. The alien who resides with you shall be to you as the citizen among you; you shall love the alien as yourself, for you were aliens in the land of Egypt; I am the Lord your God."

I thought *alien* was a strange word. It reminded me of little green men from Mars, rather than refugees fleeing for their lives.

Then Reverend Dixon had challenged the entire congregation to help. Mom had signed up to be an English tutor for Mrs. Alwan and for Dad to provide dental services for the entire family.

I was all set to be Noura's seventh-grade student ambassador, but it didn't seem like enough. My family was wealthy, safe, and secure, while hers had lost nearly everything. I imagined our first meeting. *Hi, I'm Jordyn, and I hold the state record in the 100 fly.* I wondered if Noura knew anything about competitive swimming, or if she'd ask, *What is this 100 fly? A giant bug?* I had never been friends with a Syrian or with a Muslim before. I had lots of questions, but my parents didn't seem to know any more about Islam than the things I'd read in a textbook—they believed in one God, read the Qur'an, and obeyed the teachings of their prophet, Muhammad.

"Oh, I almost forgot," Mom said. She reached into her large handbag and pulled out a teddy bear. "I brought this for Ismail."

I blurted out, "That bear was supposed to be for our baby, wasn't it?" As soon as I said it, I wished I could take the words back.

Mom clutched the bear with a wistful look on her face. "If I ever get pregnant again, we'll buy a new one."

I looked down at my shoes, feeling even more awful and guilty than I usually did. If only Mom had been home resting, instead of sitting on a hard bleacher, maybe things would be different. "Sorry, I shouldn't have mentioned the baby." I pulled an envelope from my back pocket and turned away from Mom. "I forgot to leave Noura's letter. I'll be right back."

Once I was safely inside Noura's room, I tucked the letter underneath her pillow and took a deep, shuddering breath. The pain in Mom's eyes had caused a flood of horrible memories about the best/worst day of my life. I had been chasing my dream to set a new state record for eleven- to twelve-year-olds in the 100 fly.

Once I dove into the pool, I was aware of only one thing—being first to the wall. My body moved in a wavelike motion—I was Ariel without the tail. I attacked the water with my arms, while my kicks propelled me faster than ever before. I felt invincible that day.

When I came up for air, Coach B was jumping around like Tigger—her short, spiked hair stood on end. Nobody had to tell me I'd set a new state record. I could feel it. My eyes scanned the bleachers for my parents. I knew they would be as excited as I was, but I didn't see them. I searched the bleachers a second time. And a third. My parents would never leave such an important meet without telling me. Never. There had to be an emergency. I was shaking even before my friend Lea's dad explained something terrible had happened. Something that was even more life-changing than my name on the scoreboard: JORDYN JOHNSON 56.49.

While I was breaking a state record, Mom had a miscarriage. I haven't swum well since, and I don't know how to fix my swimming—or my mom.

CHAPTER THREE

❧ NOURA ❧

Monday, February 6, 2017

Ammar slouched beside me, tapping his foot as I stared out the window of the school office, wondering . . . wondering how we could be the luckiest and unluckiest family in the world. Before the war, we were blessed to have everything: a large extended family, friends, stylish clothes, toys, and a home in one of the most beautiful cities in the world. *Lucky.* Then war took it all away and we lost everything, except for our lives. *Unlucky.* Now we'd been taken in by America, while so many others had been turned away. *Lucky?* I wasn't so sure.

I wanted nothing more than to fly back to our new apartment and into Mama's warm, sweet-smelling kitchen. She and Ismail had been baking pistachio-filled *maamoul* cookies for our neighbor Mrs. Muamba. She'd shown us how to use the mailbox when she'd seen us standing around, looking confused. A refugee herself, from the Congo, she'd

shared helpful tips about the apartment complex and promised to introduce Baba and Mama to another refugee family
who'd recently moved from Afghanistan. I sighed and shifted
my gaze to my lap, my fingers playing with the brooch that
fastened my maroon hijab.

Baba had wanted us to begin school as soon as possible, to
get into a schedule and adjust to life in America. Amani,
who'd met us at the airport, had visited twice, once to show
us around our new neighborhood, which included a trip to
the grocery store. The immense, brightly lit building, filled
with aisle after aisle of colorful packages, had taken my
breath away. I still couldn't believe that in America there
were entire sections devoted to cereal and chips! Mama had
not been impressed and had asked where the fruits and vegetables were.

That afternoon, while Ammar and I had sucked sticky
tricolored Popsicles and watched *Toy Story* with Ismail,
Amani had sat at the dinette table with my parents. I'd overheard fragments of their conversation: *President Trump . . .
ban on Muslims entering the United States . . . legally challenging the law in court.* It sounded like the president and many
politicians didn't want Muslims coming to America. I wondered what that meant for us, and it left an unsettled feeling
in my stomach.

The next time she'd visited, Amani had driven us to school to meet Mrs. Maisel, the guidance counselor, and take a series of tests. Ammar hadn't missed a single question on the math exam and I'd done okay too. English was easier to understand on the page, but when people spoke quickly, with their short, flat accents, it was harder to keep up.

Lost in thought that this was my first day of school, I didn't notice the large pair of sneakers approach until Ammar poked me with his elbow. My gaze traveled up a long pair of legs and a yellow-and-white-print shirt to a smiling face framed by shoulder-length blond hair. She was wearing a necklace made from a silver coin with a fish in the center, and was one of the tallest girls I'd ever seen. I knew immediately who she was: the girl who'd left the note underneath my pillow.

> Dear Noura,
>
> Welcome to Tampa!
> My name is Jordyn Johnson, and
> I'll be your student ambassador at
> Bayshore Middle School. In case
> you're not familiar with student
> ambassadors, I'll be helping you

find your classes and having lunch
with you.

The first thing you should know
about me is I'm six feet tall. The
other girls on the swim team call
me "G" for Giant. Being so tall
is great for swimming, but not
so great when I'm shopping for
clothes.

I guess we'll be seeing a lot of
each other because my mom will
be one of your mom's English
tutors, and my dad will be your
family dentist. FYI, his teeth are
white enough to blind you. He's a
fanatic about stuff like fluoride and
flossing.

I hope you like the floral quilt
on your bed — orchids. It's from
Pottery Barn Teen. I wanted
to make sure your room didn't
look like an old lady's, and the
turquoise, pink, and yellow colors
remind me of Florida.

And one last thing — I've never met
anyone from Syria and don't know
much about Islam, so I hope to
learn a lot from you.
See you at school soon,

Jordyn

"Jordyn?" I said uncertainly.

The girl's smile widened, revealing a gap between her two front teeth. "Yes. And you're Noura and Ammar, right?"

"Yes," I said.

"Welcome to Bayshore Middle School," she said with a smile.

"Thank you," I replied, while Ammar nodded, as quiet and solid as the blocks of wood he built with.

Jordyn paused and pointed at my brooch. "I love your peacock. It's really colorful."

"My father gave it to me on my ninth birthday," I said, rubbing the shiny enamel with my thumb. It was one of the few things I had been able to keep from home.

"My sister loves anything to do with birds," Ammar said, and then sealed his lips shut in a way I knew all too well.

As I nodded, the school secretary called out, "Good to see you, Jordyn. Are you ready to be a student ambassador?"

"Yes, Mrs. Jackson," Jordyn said, waving to her on our way out the door.

The next fifteen minutes passed in a blur as Jordyn led us through the school. I struggled to keep up with her long strides while trying to remember where my locker was as we passed classrooms, the library, gymnasium, and cafeteria. In Kilis, we'd only had one room that served as the entire school, and in Aleppo, my all-girls school had been a quarter this size, before it had been flattened by a bomb.

"I'm not in your homeroom," Jordyn said, "but we're in math and social studies together, which is next. Just follow the map in your folder and I'll meet you outside."

"Class, please welcome Noura and Ammar," said Mr. Fowler, raising his pale bushy eyebrows and spreading his arms wide. "I'm pleased they're joining us. Having them in class should broaden everyone's worldview."

I muffled a smile at the teacher's name. *Fowler.* It reminded me of the English word *fowl*: a domesticated bird used for eggs and meat. He kind of looked like a chicken, chest out, pacing the room as if seeking corn to peck.

After muttering our hello, Ammar and I followed Jordyn to our seats, and the girl sitting in front of me turned and smiled. I smiled too, admiring the deep red henna designs that decorated her hands.

"I'm Daksha," she whispered.

"Hi," I whispered back. "I love your henna."

"Thanks." She grinned and turned to face our teacher.

Mr. Fowler stood at the front of the room. "For our new students, I want to share what we've covered in class so far. At the beginning of the year, we examined the foundation of the US government, the history of our political process, and then analyzed the components of the constitution. For the next few months, we'll study the roles, rights, and responsibilities of US citizens, with a special focus on civic engagement and active participation in our political system."

I exchanged a worried look with Ammar. I didn't know any of what he had just said. We had a lot of catching up to do.

A girl with a mop of tangled blond hair raised her hand, waving to get Mr. Fowler's attention.

"Yes, Penny?" he asked.

"So, what do you mean by participating in the political system? Could it be like holding a demonstration? I'm thinking of the Native American groups who protested building the oil pipeline across their land."

"That's a good example," Mr. Fowler said. "One of the things we take pride in in America is the ability of everyday people to make a difference. That means being able to vote, serve on a jury, or participate in a protest."

Mr. Fowler pivoted and wrote a word on the board in sharp strokes. "Citizen," he said, adjusting the jacket of his brown-checked suit. "What makes a citizen, you may ask. Well, babies born in the United States are granted automatic citizenship. But for those not born here, there is a defined process to becoming a citizen, which is neither easy nor fast."

I focused on the word. *Citizen*. My passport said I was a citizen of Syria. It was the country where my family had lived for generations; where Baba's family had been in the hotel and construction business, and Mama's brothers ran a successful bakery. It was all gone now, turned to dust. Our downfall had begun in a school, just like this one, in the city of Daraa. A group of boys had written anti-government graffiti on their school wall. They were quickly arrested and tortured, and one was murdered. After that it didn't matter if you were a citizen of Syria. If you did not agree with the president, you would be killed.

"Noura, pay attention," grumbled Ammar. "He's giving a test next week."

I ducked my head, embarrassed. I couldn't help it, my

mind tended to wander. Ammar called me birdbrain when I frustrated him beyond his patience.

"There will be a group immigration project due in six weeks, and all research topics have to be approved by me," announced Mr. Fowler, rubbing his palms together. "And bonus points if you unearth a piece of history or a fact that I'm unfamiliar with."

Behind me, a red-haired, freckle-faced boy muttered underneath his breath, "Immigrants are terrorists."

Eyes wide, I looked at Ammar. Did the boy really say what I thought he had? My brother stiffened, a frown tugging at his scar. Jordyn whipped around to glare at the boy. The other kids who sat close enough to hear looked away from us.

"Since we have thirty kids," Mr. Fowler continued, "you'll work in groups of three."

Jordyn furiously waved her hand in the air.

"Yes, Jordyn?" said Mr. Fowler.

"I'd like to work with Noura," she said. "And Ammar too."

"Great," he said. "We have our first group."

When I turned to give Jordyn a grateful smile, the girl sitting to her right scowled at me. Her short chestnut hair bounced as she leaned toward Jordyn, and her beaded bracelet clanked against her desk. "G, you were supposed to work on the project with Lea and me," she said. "You know, swim team sisters—Jordyn, Bailey, Lea."

"Yeah," grumbled the girl sitting in front of Jordyn. She turned and crossed her arms over a T-shirt that said, SWIM LIKE THERE'S FLAN AT THE FINISH LINE, and raised one inky-black eyebrow.

I was impressed. I had always wished I could raise just one eyebrow and look at people in a superior way, but my eyebrows had never cooperated.

"Oh . . . gosh, guys," Jordyn blurted, looking from one girl to the other. "I totally wanted to work with you . . . but I . . . I thought I should work with Noura and Ammar since I'm their student ambassador."

Lea and Bailey both gave Jordyn irritated looks, and she responded with a sheepish smile. Even I knew they were stuck with the awful boy—the one with the red hair.

Dhuhr prayer was going to begin at 12:46 and if I hurried, I'd finish by 1:00, well before lunch was over at 1:35. Ammar and I needed to find a spot to pray and fast. I flew to the girls' bathroom and quickly removed my hijab. Without thinking twice, I recited *Bismillah-ir-Rahman-ir-Rahim, in the name of God the merciful and compassionate,* an invocation given to Allah whenever you begin something. I rolled up my sleeves and quickly washed my hands and face, then along my ears and arms. Next I kicked off my sandals and awkwardly lifted my foot into the sink just as the bathroom door opened with a groan.

"Oh my God, what *is* she doing?" said a horrified voice.

The revulsion in the girl's voice filled me with confusion as water ran over my toes. I looked in the mirror and saw a group of girls behind me. I recognized them right away. Jordyn stood a head taller than the others, a strange look on her face.

My cheeks felt hot and my body stiffened as the knowledge I was doing something terribly wrong spread over me like thick, sticky honey.

Lea's dark eyes narrowed. "That's so gross," she muttered.

Tongue-tied, I stood there. Words of explanation pooled in my mouth but wouldn't come out. I pinched the inside of my wrist. The pain sent me into motion and I jerked my foot out of the sink and turned to face them.

CHAPTER FOUR

❧ JORDYN ❧

Monday, February 6, 2017

My friends Lea and Bailey kept staring at Noura. Honestly, I was mystified. I'd been to the Alwans' apartment, and there was no reason she couldn't take a bath at home.

Noura's cheeks were flushed—she was embarrassed, and I wasn't sure what to do. There was nothing in the student ambassador handbook about bathroom etiquette. Finally, I muttered, "Girls, quit staring."

"It is okay," Noura said, her eyes not quite meeting mine. She dried her foot on a paper towel. "I am making *wudu*."

Bailey rolled her bright hazel eyes. "Wow, that really clears things up."

I nudged Bailey with my elbow. I wasn't sure if making *wudu* was a Syrian custom, or a Muslim one, but either way there was no reason to be rude.

"I am cleansing before prayer," Noura explained.

"Oh. Oh . . . I pray all the time. Praying is totally normal. Totally. I've . . . I've just never thought about washing my feet first . . . in the sink." I turned to Lea and Bailey. "See, everything's cool here."

Lea shrugged. "Mami says cleanliness is next to godliness, but this seems a little extreme."

Noura held her head high. "I can explain more during lunch. Right now, I need to go. My brother is waiting for me."

Before leaving, Noura covered her hair with her hijab. I had told Bailey and Lea to stop staring, but I was curious too.

I hurried through the cafeteria line and bought a Cuban sandwich and a huge chocolate chip cookie. Lea and Bailey had both packed their lunches and grabbed a table for us in the courtyard.

As soon as I sat down, Lea said, "I know you're Noura's student ambassador, and it's your job to help her, but it's *all* your fault we got stuck working with Nick Sawyer."

I broke my cookie into thirds and put the pieces onto napkins for my friends. "I'm sorry you have to partner with Nick, but his stupid comment about terrorists really ticked me off. I wanted to be sure Noura and Ammar knew they have friends here."

"It's not like I agree with Nick or anything," Bailey said, "but maybe he has a point."

Lea drained her juice box and wiped away a grape mustache. "My last name is Rodriguez, and my *abuela* speaks mostly Spanish." She wadded her napkin into a ball. "Oh, and we're planning a *quinceañera* for my older sister. What do you have against immigrants, anyway?"

"It's not the same," Bailey mumbled. "Cuban immigrants aren't terrorists."

I put my sandwich down and stared at Bailey. "That sounds kind of prejudiced."

"I am not prejudiced," Bailey said, but then she pointed a cheese stick at me. "Noura is dressed like Mary in a Christmas pageant. The Bible doesn't tell girls what to wear. I'll bet the Qur'an doesn't either."

I shrugged. "I have no idea what the Qur'an says about clothing. Heck, I don't even know what the Bible says about clothing. Do you?"

Bailey's face turned as red as my favorite bathing suit.

"Well, at our church, the Virgin Mary always has her head covered," Lea said.

I was about to agree with Lea on the Virgin Mary thing when she nudged my calf with her foot. It was a reminder to be extra nice to Bailey because her older brother had been killed in Afghanistan. We'd all loved Bryan. He'd been our first swim coach. "Guys, I watched a documentary at church about the refugees, and I can't stop thinking about it. Kids— kids just like us are scared and hungry. If you'd seen it, I bet you'd want to help them too."

Bailey rolled her eyes. "Maybe, or maybe not. Muslims set the roadside bomb that killed Bryan."

"I'm sorry about Bryan," I said softly. "You know I am, but Noura and Ammar didn't have anything to do with that bomb."

Lea put her thumb and index finger together and dragged them across her lips like a zipper. From the corner of my eye, I saw Noura and Ammar standing beside me, and felt a prickly heat spread across my face. "Uh . . . uh, hi." I gestured toward the empty chairs at our table. "Want to join us?"

Noura and Ammar sat down and unwrapped their lunches—some kind of fried pie with meat inside. If Noura was still embarrassed about washing her feet, or had overheard us talking about roadside bombs, she was good at hiding it. "Those look delicious. What are they?"

"*Kibbe,*" Noura answered. "Would you like to try one?"

"Sure."

Carefully, she passed it over to me. I took a bite and tasted lamb, onions, cinnamon, and other spices that I didn't recognize. "It's delicious," I said, so delicious I could have eaten a whole plate full of them.

"I'll trade you an empanada for a *kibbe*," Lea said. I was relieved she was making an effort to be nice and wasn't holding a grudge about having to work with Nick. She really didn't like him.

"What kind of meat is inside?" Noura asked.

Lea shook her head. "Vegetarian. They're stuffed with black beans and plantains."

I looked down at my sandwich. I always used to pack my lunch, but since Mom's miscarriage, she hardly went to the grocery store. Now Dad left money on the kitchen counter instead. I hadn't touched half my sandwich, but didn't offer it to Noura or Ammar. I knew pork was taboo for Muslims and hoped I wasn't grossing them out.

"So, what's up with putting your feet in the sink?" Bailey asked.

Noura smiled shyly. "Before praying, we wash our arms, feet, and face."

"But why?" Bailey asked.

"Well . . ." Noura paused as if nobody had ever asked such a question before. "We want to be clean in body and in spirit before talking to God."

"That makes total sense," I said. "It reminds me of being baptized. How often do you do it?"

"We make *wudu* and pray five times a day," Ammar answered.

Noura looked at her brother with soft, sad eyes. "Using water also cools you down and takes away the heat of anger."

He frowned at her, which made his scar pucker. I averted my eyes from the right side of his face, wondering what had happened to him and if making *wudu* and praying had helped him deal with it. My scars were on the inside, where they were easier to hide—I was glad about that.

CHAPTER FIVE

⪦ NOURA ⪧

Saturday, February 11, 2017

I volunteered to stir the pot of steaming lentil soup while Mama put Ismail down for a nap and Baba sorted through a stack of printouts. It was nice to be in the small, cozy apartment after a long, stressful week at school. I peered out the window, spying the bird feeder Ammar had crafted from a plastic milk bottle, nails, and wood. Even though he would never admit it, Ammar had constructed the bird feeder for Ismail and me. I loved showing them the incredible variety of birds that dropped by for lunch: bossy bluebirds, tiny yellow-breasted goldfinches, gentle wrens, brown-and-white thrashers, chatty chickadees, iridescent grackles, and many others.

For a moment, it even felt like home. Or what home had been like before war had enveloped Aleppo. As soon as the bombs began to fall, the beautiful songbirds at Baba's hotel had stopped singing or laying eggs. And thankfully, before

Beit Zafran had been destroyed, I'd set them free—free to fly away and find a new home where they could thrive and be happy. Baba hadn't even been angry when I told him.

Though Jordyn was guiding us, Ammar and I had realized that school in America was very different than it had been in Syria. Plus, trying to keep up with all the new English words flying past my head like dive-bombing hummingbirds had made my brain ache a little.

Now as I watched Baba read one job posting after the other, I desperately searched for a joke or something interesting I could spring on him to smooth the wrinkles on his forehead. No jokes came to mind, or any riddles either. Perhaps I could tell him about our upcoming social studies quiz, or our group project. I'd hoped Ammar and I could meet with Jordyn today to get started on our project, but she'd mentioned she had a swim meet.

Before I could bring it up, Baba's cell phone rang. He ran to the kitchen counter and snatched it up, not wanting to wake Ismail.

"Hello," he said, then listened intently, his face creasing into a pleased smile. "Yes, I can come in for an interview on Friday," he added, picking up a pen to scribble down the address.

Excitement mingled with relief flowed through me. Baba

had applied to over sixty jobs and had been on two interviews, but nothing had come of them. "An interview? That's
so great," I said as he hung up.

"It's at a hotel," he said, standing taller.

"Are you going to be the manager?" I asked.

"No, *habibti*," he chuckled. "The position is for a
bellhop."

Bellhop? I thought. *You ring a bell while hopping?*
"What's that?"

"Someone who helps the guests with their luggage," he
explained.

"What?" I gasped. "Do they know who you are? That you
ran one of the best hotels in Aleppo?"

Baba sighed. "That was a different time and place, my
love. I have to work my way up in America. And frankly, any
honest job that takes care of our family's needs is a good
job—full of blessings from Allah."

I nodded, not wanting him to feel bad. I'd heard him and
Mama talking about the $2,718 they owed the American
government for the cost of our travel to the United States.
The debt weighed heavily upon him, and he wanted to pay
it back as soon as possible.

But still, I couldn't imagine him carrying anyone's luggage. Back in Aleppo, Baba had been renowned for managing

Beit Zafran, one of the city's finest hotels. He and his cousins had renovated an old, run-down mansion near the city's most important historical sites: the Great Mosque, the Citadel, and the sprawling souk, which had been my favorite place to shop with Mama.

They'd transformed the mansion into a five-star property with gleaming wooden panels, hand-painted tiles, and plush carpets. Guests from all over the world arrived through golden metal gates and were treated like royalty. In addition to their luxurious suites, they relaxed in the gardens, ate at the award-winning restaurant, and lounged in the courtyard. The courtyard was my favorite place, where I'd sit on cushioned seats after I fed the songbirds.

It was such a peaceful space, soothed by the sounds of the fountain, the air heavy with the scent of orange blossoms from the citrus trees, along with jasmine and roses. Baba had been at the hotel's helm, graciously conversing in multiple languages, making them feel at home. But then war had come to Aleppo, and after an onslaught of bombing, Baba's beloved hotel had been reduced to rubble . . .

The front door swung open, pulling me back from my bittersweet memories. Ammar walked in all sweaty with his hair ruffled and grass stains on his long shorts.

"How was practice?" Baba asked eagerly.

"Yes, how was it?" I echoed, not particularly interested in football, or soccer, as they called it here. Ammar had explained that in America, they had their own version of football, played with a ball with pointy ends. We were all relieved to see Ammar smile. Mama, in particular, had started crying and hidden her face when Ammar casually mentioned he'd decided to coach the little kids in our apartment building. Three of the boys were Mrs. Muamba's sons, another an Afghan refugee, and then two other kids rounded out the team. This was the first time since coming to America that Ammar had voluntarily left his room.

"Practice was good," Ammar said, grabbing a glass of water. "Some of the little ones have more enthusiasm than skill, but they'll get better."

After draining the glass, he collapsed on the floor in front of the television and switched it on. Because of Baba, it was fixed to a news station. Ammar picked up the remote to change the channel, but Baba held up his hand. "No, wait," he said as the words BREAKING NEWS flashed on the screen.

A newscaster with bright red lips and a serious tone to her voice stared back at us. "In another defeat for President Trump, the appeals court in the state of Washington has refused to reinstate the Muslim ban." The camera panned to a guest sitting beside her, Emily Wang—legal director of the American Civil Liberties Union, Washington Office. "Ms. Wang, what are your thoughts?"

"We applaud the Washington State Appeals Court decision," Ms. Wang said. "The president's Muslim travel ban is not only unconstitutional, it violates American values and has taken a great toll on innocent individuals. It has ripped apart families in our state and across the country."

"What is she saying? Muslim what?" came Mama's worried voice. She'd put Ismail to sleep and was standing in the hallway.

"Nothing, my dear, don't worry about it," Baba said.

Mama's lips tightened. "Don't pretend to keep me from worrying. I remember the protestors at the airport."

Baba looked anxiously at us and cleared his throat. "You're right, it is something. It appears that America's president doesn't want Muslims to come here. But many American people don't agree. They are fighting against his law in the courts. They say his Muslim ban goes against what Americans believe."

"But he is the *president*," said Mama, her eyes wide. "He controls the country and his words and actions will bring anger and discontent."

"It's okay, Mama," said Ammar in a soothing voice as he

rose to take her hand. "The American president is not like that dog Bashar al-Assad who killed his own people and destroyed Syria to keep power."

"Ammar, watch your language," admonished our father.

I hid a smile. Baba did not approve of bad language, even for an evil monster like the Syrian president Bashar al-Assad.

CHAPTER SIX

✸ JORDYN ✸

Saturday, February 11, 2017

As soon as I saw the dark circles under Mom's eyes, I knew she hadn't slept at all. She was in the kitchen making my usual breakfast before a swim meet: scrambled eggs, bacon, toast, and oatmeal. "Breakfast of champions coming right up," she said.

I shrugged, staring out the window at water that seemed to go on forever—Tampa Bay. I liked our condo being on the seventh floor. It wasn't too high up, or too close to the ground.

"Bay's calm," Mom said. "Good day for boating. I'll bet a lot of people will be out on the water."

I wished I were one of them. A ride on Dad's boat up the Hillsborough River, or over to St. Pete, would be a lot more fun than a swim meet, though I never used to feel that way.

"Jordyn, eggs are ready," Mom said. I grabbed a plate, wishing she had washed her hair and put on nice clothes. Instead, she was wearing a T-shirt all stretched out from when she was pregnant. I knew what the other moms would whisper as soon as they saw her. *Poor Lori Johnson. She hasn't been the same since she lost the baby.*

Mom scooped scrambled eggs onto my plate. "Sorry, the bacon's a little burned. I can't seem to focus."

I carried my breakfast over to the table and pushed the eggs around with my fork. Mom sighed. "Jordyn, honey, stop playing with your eggs."

I forced myself to take a couple of bites. "Mom, you don't have to go. Dad can take me, or I can catch a ride with Lea."

Mom hugged her stomach. "Don't be silly," she said in a trembling voice. "We've never missed one of your meets. I'm looking forward to it."

I wasn't looking forward to swimming any more than Mom was looking forward to watching me, but I didn't know how to tell her without making things worse.

The Nyad Aquatics Center was named after a long-distance swimmer, Diana Nyad. She's famous for swimming from Cuba to Florida without a shark cage. I used to think of the NAC as my second home. Before Bailey's brother, Bryan, joined the army, he used to work there. Sometimes I can still hear his voice. "Hey, G! You keep growing, you're gonna be taller than me." I always laughed when he said that, because

I was already taller than him. Now the NAC was full of painful memories for Bailey, and for me.

After changing into my lucky Speedo and favorite swim cap, I stowed my duffel bag on deck. It held everything I might possibly need: three towels, two pairs of goggles, two swim caps, a parka, and slides. I breathed in the scent of chlorine and zeroed in on lane four. Lea would be swimming beside me in lane five, and Bailey was in lane eight.

I turned and scanned the bleachers, looking for Mom and Dad. They were sitting in their usual spot about halfway up. Everything was the way it was supposed to be, only Mom and I had changed.

Lea stood beside me. *"Tranquila,"* she said.

"I am relaxed."

Lea arched her right eyebrow. I've never been able to do that, but Lea's good at it. "G, you can't fool me. We've been swimming together for too long."

Lea and I had started competitive swimming when we were seven. The butterfly became our favorite stroke because we were obsessed with Ariel and *The Little Mermaid.*

Coach headed toward us, stopping to check on each swimmer. When it was my turn, she put her hand on my shoulder. "Your skin is clammy. Are you feeling okay?"

"Just a little nervous."

Coach stood toe to toe with me, peering into my eyes. "Don't let holding a state record mess with your head. I need you to swim your heart out."

I looked away from Coach and up at Mom. It wasn't the state record that was messing with my head—or with my heart. It was like the swimmer I used to be had died, but nobody had realized it yet.

A few minutes later, I climbed on the starting block, waiting for the beep. I felt the kind of lonely you feel in a crowd. I dove in, but my mind was a million miles away. As my arms rose out of the water, I took a breath, kicking twice for each stroke. I wondered if Mom was okay, or if like me, she was reliving what happened.

On the second lap, *the old* G took the lead. I thought maybe I had a shot at winning, but my arms and legs grew heavy. I needed to breathe on every stroke. After the third turn, I totally ran out of steam. When I touched the wall and pushed up my goggles, Coach was running toward Lea. *Lea had won*, and she'd tied my state record!

While Coach pumped her fist in the air, I was stunned. Something was seriously *wrong* with me. I took a couple of ragged breaths. When I stopped shaking, I swam over and congratulated Lea. She had never swum faster than me in competition before and whispered, "G, what happened?"

I blinked back tears, realizing on top of everything else, I was jealous of my best friend. "Nothing happened. You swam a great race, Bailey came in fifth, and I'm having a bad day."

After the swim meet, I was lying on my bed, staring at the fish swimming around in my aquarium, when Dad knocked. "Jordyn, can I come in?"

I really wanted to be left alone, but I knew he would keep checking back until I agreed to talk to him.

Dad pulled my desk chair over beside the bed and sat down. He stared at his hands, clasped between his knees. "Honey, I know what happened today hurts. Nobody likes to come up short."

I shrugged.

Dad ran his hand through his thick sand-colored hair. "None of us are the same since the miscarriage, and we're all handling it differently. Your mom hardly wants to leave the condo, but it makes me feel better to go to work. You've been quieter than usual, and your swimming's a little off. I'm sorry for not paying more attention."

"It's okay." I brushed tears off my cheeks with the back of my hand. The way I had swum was more than *a little off*, but I couldn't tell Dad the truth or he'd know what a horrible person I was. I hadn't really wanted Mom to have a baby. When I was younger, I wanted a baby like Lea's sister, Gaby, but I was already twelve when Mom got pregnant, and suddenly, she was paying less attention to me and obsessed with what color to paint the nursery. I wondered if somehow, my resentment had caused Mom's miscarriage, and not swimming well was my punishment.

Dad reached over and ruffled my hair. "Hang in there, kiddo. Mom has an appointment with a therapist, and we're gonna get through this." He stood up to leave. "I think you should stop by Coach Barnes's office. She'll know how to get your swimming back on track."

Coach Barnes—I grabbed on to her name like a lifeline. Maybe she knew how I could get my confidence back.

CHAPTER SEVEN

⚞ NOURA ⚟

Monday, February 13, 2017

There it was—the door to social studies class, where our exam would start in minutes. "Come on," muttered Ammar. "We don't want to be late."

I followed, feeling a little queasy. Instead of soft, gentle butterflies floating inside my stomach, angry crows with sharp beaks and claws were building their nests to make me miserable. I had wanted to skip breakfast, but Mama insisted Ammar and I have a healthy meal before our big social studies exam. Not wanting to hurt her feelings, I'd filled my plate with eggs, stewed beans, cheese, lamb sausage, olives, and bread with fig jam. My stomach groaned again and I tried my best to ignore it.

I was so tired from staying up late that Mama had to wake me three times for *fajr* prayers that morning. All I'd wanted was to snuggle into my blanket and go back to sleep. Feeling guilty, I'd asked Allah to at least get 75 percent of the questions correct. I'd studied the whole weekend, memorizing facts and figures. The concepts I couldn't understand I researched on the internet. Ammar had thought I was going overboard, but I'd told him this was important—it was our first exam in America, and I wanted to get off on the right foot.

I followed Ammar down the hall and into Mr. Fowler's classroom. Right away, I spotted a blond head bent toward two others, one chestnut brown, the other inky black. It was Jordyn, whispering with her friends Lea and Bailey. Snatches of their conversation floated over to me.

"You just had a stroke of bad luck," Lea said.

"Exactly," Bailey agreed. "We all go through rough spots now and then. You'll kick butt next time and probably break your own state record."

Jordyn sighed and shrugged, a look of resignation on her face. I turned away and meandered toward my desk, suddenly wishing I were back at school in Aleppo. I'd be sitting with Maryam, Yasmeen, and Rania, gossiping about who we thought would win *Arab Idol* that season.

"Good luck," whispered Daksha, the girl who sat in front of me.

"Thanks," I said. "Good luck to you too."

"I never know how much to study," Daksha said, a frown

creasing her pretty features. "Of course, my mom says not enough."

I laughed, my heart lightening. "Mine too!"

We gave each other a conspiratorial smile, and I pulled out my pencil case and study sheet for a final review.

"That's so cool," Jordyn said, sliding into a seat beside me. "How do you write so small?"

"Oh," I said, lifting up the page where I'd neatly written out my notes, color-coded by topic and laid out in a series of squares. "This is how my friends and I used to write our study notes. My handwriting isn't nearly as small as my best friend Maryam's." The memory of green-eyed Maryam sent a pang of anxiety through me. I didn't want to think about her. *About what had happened to her.*

"Can I take a quick look at it?" Thankfully, Jordyn dispelled the dark thoughts swirling in my mind. "I had trouble studying last night."

With a sense of pride, I handed my notes to her. Daksha turned around to look, and even Lea and Bailey peered down at the sheet in awe.

"My mother would be so impressed," sighed Daksha.

"It is pretty cool," Bailey said, looking both impressed and a little aghast.

"Thanks," I said, and held up the bright rainbow-colored eraser Baba had bought for me at the office supply store. I'd tagged along when he'd gone to purchase construction paper and colored pencils for one of Ammar's art projects. "I brought this in case of many mistakes."

"All right, everyone take your seats," Mr. Fowler squawked from the front of the room. "And put away your cell phones and review materials."

Before lining up my pencil and eraser, I took back the study sheet and slipped it into my backpack. Beside me, Ammar slouched in his chair, arms folded over his chest.

"Good luck," I whispered to him.

"You too," he said. "But you've studied enough for both of us. You don't need any luck."

I felt a surge of confidence and sat up straighter as Mr. Fowler placed a copy of the quiz on my desk.

Before starting, I closed my eyes, took a deep, calming breath, and whispered, *"Bismillah-ir-Rahman-ir-Raheem."* I gave my peacock brooch a quick rub for good luck and picked up my pencil to read the first question.

1. **Explain the three different ways of becoming a United States citizen.**

I knew the answer! I carefully wrote it down and moved to number two.

When I finished, I sat back and checked the clock. *Ten minutes. That's all the time I needed to complete the quiz!* With fifteen minutes still to go, I grew fidgety. I twiddled my thumbs, sneaking glances at the other kids who were still hard at work. Penny, the girl with unruly hair, sat ahead of me, biting her nails.

A sniffle caught my attention. In the second row, a pudgy boy with sad, dark eyes wiped his nose. He wasn't paying attention to his paper at all. Mr. Fowler walked over and bent down beside his desk. "Joel," he whispered. "Would you like to take a break?"

The boy shook his head and continued to stare at his paper. With a pat on Joel's shoulder, Mr. Fowler walked back to the front of the room.

I wondered what was wrong with Joel, but not wanting to pry, I quickly looked away and over at Ammar. He'd turned the page and was working on the last set of questions.

I peered to the right and squinted in surprise. Jordyn sat completely still with her eyes closed, gripping her pencil. Aside from her flushed cheeks, she was as pale as the bellies of fish Grandfather had caught on his boating trips to the Euphrates. Had she had a mind freeze? That sometimes happened to me, but not very often. Then I heard her short, labored gasps. Sweat pooled along her upper lip. "Jordyn, are you all right?" I whispered.

She blinked and stared at me with eyes the dark blue of a stormy sea. Shocked, I recognized her emotions because they mirrored my own . . . *panic, whenever I was near water.* Before I could say more, she blinked again, as if rising from an abyss where she'd battled terrible beasts.

"I'm fine," she said, color returning to her face. "It's nothing."

"No talking!" ordered Mr. Fowler. I bit my lip and turned back toward my desk.

After Mr. Fowler collected our quizzes, he flipped through all of them. "Only two students answered the extra credit question," he said, looking a little disappointed. "Put on your thinking caps: *How has climate change contributed to a worldwide refugee crisis?*"

When no one responded, he said, "Ammar, would you like to tell the class about this phenomenon?"

Ammar's jaw clenched and his scar turned white. I raised my hand, hoping Mr. Fowler would ask me instead. From behind me, someone muttered, "What a know-it-all."

Ignoring him, I blurted out, "My father told me that climate change caused years of drought, forcing over a million Syrian farmers to leave their land and move to the cities.

They suffered from unemployment and abuse by the government. Many of them joined protests that led to our civil war, forcing us to become refugees."

"No such thing as climate change. It's just fake news," said Nick.

"You're an idiot," Penny cried. "Climate change is true and Floridians better fight it, or we're gonna end up underwater when the polar ice melts."

"Penny, no name-calling," admonished Mr. Fowler. "But to add to what Noura said, climate change is causing severe weather pattern swings around the world. It's causing people to leave their homes and search for new ones—creating a refugee crisis."

"See." Penny smirked, crossing her arms over her chest.

"Great job keeping up with current events," Mr. Fowler said, slipping a rubber band around the stack of test papers. "Noura and Ammar's family have been directly affected by the refugee crisis, but I expect everyone in my class to keep up with world events. One of my goals is to develop informed global citizens."

"Yeah, whatever," mumbled Nick.

Stung, this time I couldn't help but grumble, "It's easy to ignore current events when they don't personally affect you . . . or your family."

CHAPTER EIGHT

❧ JORDYN ❧

Wednesday, February 15, 2017

After practice, I stopped by Coach's office. When I knocked on the doorframe, she looked up from behind her desk. "Come on in, Jordyn. I just need a sec to finish this email."

Since the last time I'd dropped by, Coach had added to her book collection. I wandered over and examined the shelves crammed with how-to manuals, biographies of swimmers, and photos of past swim teams. I was drawn to a picture of Coach with her arm slung around Bryan's shoulders. I dusted it off with the hem of my T-shirt.

When I looked up, Coach was watching me. "I'm not much of a housekeeper," she admitted, "but Bryan was one of a kind."

I placed their picture back on the bookshelf. "I miss Bryan, and it has to be a thousand times worse for Bailey. He was just so young."

Coach nodded, her brown eyes reflecting my sadness. "I call them *out-of-order deaths*. When an older person dies, they've lived a full life, but when it's a young person, we feel like they've been cheated."

I took a seat in front of Coach's desk, staring at my flip-flops. "I'm in a slump."

"Any idea why?"

I sighed, not sure of how much to tell her, or if the way I'd freaked out in social studies was related. "My family's sort of a mess since Mom's miscarriage."

"I understand," Coach said. She tapped a pencil on her desk a few times. "My wife had a miscarriage about five years ago. The hardest part was how people just expected us to get over it, like our loss didn't count in the same way as couples who had lost an older child."

"My mom said that too."

Coach put her pencil down and leaned toward me. "If you hadn't texted me to set up a meeting, I would've called you. My being happy for Lea doesn't mean I'm not sad for you. I would've told you that on Saturday, except I didn't think you were ready to hear it."

I kept staring at my flip-flops. "Yeah, Saturday was hard."

"I'll bet," Coach said, "and now we need a plan to get you

back on track." She marched over to the whiteboard hanging on the wall behind my chair. "I'm a visual learner, so I'm gonna write this down." She grabbed a red marker and made a list:

1. Have fun in the pool.
2. Take care of yourself (eat nutritious meals, get enough sleep, stay properly hydrated).
3. Talk about your feelings.
4. Visualize (picture yourself winning)!

With both index fingers, she pointed to the bookshelves on either side of her desk. "Every great swimmer has overcome huge setbacks. It might help if you read some of their stories."

Since both her bookshelves were overflowing, I had lots of choices. "Any recommendations?"

Coach headed over to the shelf on her right and pulled *Relentless Spirit*. "Try this one. Missy Franklin is a lot like you. She's an only child, her faith is important to her, and as you already know, she didn't swim her best at the Olympics."

I took the book from Coach's outstretched hand and hugged

it to my chest. "Thank you. Maybe Missy's story will help me. Sometimes it feels like I'm the only one not swimming well."

Coach spread her arms wide, raising a palm toward each bookshelf. "You're far from alone. And when you finish with that memoir, there are plenty more."

On my way out, I turned to tell Coach one last thing. "I always feel better after talking to you."

She flashed a wide smile, and I was pretty sure Dad had whitened her teeth. "It's like I always say, I have the best job in the world."

After biking home, I dropped my backpack by the front door and stood looking out at the boats bobbing on the bay.

"Jordyn, is that you?"

Mom was hidden from sight by the back of our cream-colored sofa, and as she sat up, a blue afghan fell to the floor.

"Yeah, I'm late because I had a meeting with Coach."

As I got closer, I noticed Mom's eyes were red and swollen. I kicked my shoes off and sat down on the opposite end of the sofa, tucking my legs underneath me. "I guess you had a hard day, huh?"

Mom stared up at the ceiling and tears leaked out the corners of her eyes. "My friend Sarah is pregnant."

I leaned forward and wrapped my arms around Mom,

trying to comfort her the same way she used to comfort me. "Should I call Dad?"

Mom shook her head against my chest. "He's working. There's no reason to disturb him."

I held her for a long time and watched the boats.

"I'm jealous," Mom whispered. "How petty is that? Sarah has been my friend for nearly twenty years, and instead of being happy for her, I'm avoiding her calls."

That was so similar to how I'd felt when Lea tied my state record that I squeezed my eyes shut to keep from crying. "I'm sorry, Mom." Those words sounded hollow, but I couldn't think of any better ones.

Mom used a wadded-up Kleenex to wipe her eyes. "I did everything right," she said softly. "I got plenty of rest, ate properly, took my vitamins, but my body didn't do what it was supposed to."

What Mom said echoed in my mind. *My body didn't do what it was supposed to.* Mine hadn't either, not at the swim meet or during the social studies test.

"As soon as I feel ready, the doctor said I can try again," Mom said.

I hoped she would have another baby, but not yet. I remembered the list Coach had written on her whiteboard. Mom and I needed to do lots of the same things. "We both need a plan to get back in shape. Since your miscarriage, we haven't been eating all that healthy. I would have never believed it, but I'm sick of pepperoni pizza."

Mom blew her nose hard and it honked. "I sound like a duck," she said, "and I'm sorry we've been eating so much takeout, but I haven't been grocery shopping."

I hopped off the sofa and padded over to the kitchen. I found some potatoes in the pantry. They were a little soft and had eyes, but I thought they were still okay. Next, I checked the freezer and found a package of green beans with almonds.

Mom wandered into the kitchen. "Need some help?"

"Yeah. How about peeling the potatoes, and I'll bike to Publix for a rotisserie chicken?"

Mom studied the potatoes as if they were rocks from outer space. "Okay," she finally said, "I can do that."

I rode my bike on the sidewalk along the bay, automatically dodging people who were jogging and rollerblading. Everyone else seemed so happy. I wondered if I looked that way to them too—carefree girl out for a late-afternoon ride—instead of who I was—a girl biking for dinner because her mom was too depressed to cook. Mom. She was never far from my thoughts these days. I thought back to our conversation in the condo. She hadn't asked about my social studies quiz, or swim practice, or my meeting with Coach. Deep inside, I knew Mom loved me, but she'd stopped paying attention. I steered my bike into the parking lot, wishing I could confess how I'd really felt about the baby, but I didn't think Mom was strong enough to deal with my problems on top of her own.

CHAPTER NINE

❧ NOURA ❧

Friday, February 17, 2017

M r. Fowler walked down the aisle, handing back our quizzes. As he neared my desk, I slouched lower in my seat, nervously running my hands along the shiny rhinestones sewn into my new jeans. I'd been so excited when I'd found them at the thrift store Mama and I had stumbled on while taking Ismail for a walk. But I was filled with self-doubt, and the rhinestones were little comfort as I scolded myself—*Noura, you are a donkey! Why did you finish the exam so quickly?* I probably hadn't read the English correctly and missed many of the questions.

With a quick wink, Mr. Fowler slid my exam across the desk. I squinted, staring down at the top right-hand corner. In bright red, it said minus three. Eighty-five percent. But with the extra credit points, my final score was 90 percent!

"Ammar," I whispered, sitting up straight and showing him my page.

"Great." He grinned, pointing to his own. Seventy-five percent.

I sat back, a warmth spreading through my body. Baba would be so proud. He and Mama would be relieved we were adjusting to life in America so quickly. Already, we'd made a home for ourselves and Baba had a job at the hotel, even though it was as a bellhop. We still missed our family, and Mama was on the phone a lot with her mother and sisters, but we'd made new friends.

Daksha turned to give me a thumbs-up, and I returned it before glancing over at Jordyn, who sat staring out the window. I caught a glimpse of her paper and saw that she had missed eight questions, leaving her with 60 percent on the exam. It shocked me. It was a barely passing score.

"Jordyn," Bailey hissed from the other side. "How'd you do?"

Jordyn blinked a few times and turned to her friend. "What?" she asked, as if she hadn't heard.

"I got a ninety-five. Just missed one. What did you get?" Lea asked.

"I didn't do so well," Jordyn said, quickly flipping her exam over and hiding behind her blond hair, as if it were a curtain.

Quickly, I looked away, not wanting Jordyn to think I was

being nosy. I could tell something was bothering her. And it wasn't just her poor performance on the exam and how anxious she'd gotten while taking it. I recognized those feelings. They were dark, chaotic emotions that pulled you under their waves, cutting off the very air you breathed. I wanted to talk to her, but I didn't know how. She was my friend, but I'd only known her for a few weeks. I didn't want her to get mad at me for prying into her business.

After school, I sat at the kitchen table with my notebook and a plate of fresh fruit Mama had cut up for snacks. "Ammar," I called. "We've got to start thinking about our social studies project."

"Yeah, I know," came his muffled voice from his bedroom.

"I know you know," I shouted, feeling a little frustrated by his lack of enthusiasm.

I didn't want to tell Baba or he would be upset, but it seemed Ammar spent more time with his models and drawings than he did with his schoolwork. Dressed in his shorts and a T-shirt, Ammar headed toward the front door with a soccer ball under his arm.

"Where are you going?" I asked, my temper rising.

"I promised the kids I'd help them with goal kicking," he said, grabbing half an apple from the plate.

"But we have work to do!" I grumbled, then lowered my voice. "And you missed afternoon prayers."

Ammar gave me a dark, mutinous look. "Who are you? The prayer police?"

I sealed my lips shut, stung by his words. It wasn't like I didn't miss a prayer now and then.

"We have the whole weekend to work on it," he added, daring me to say something. When I didn't, he slipped through the front door.

"What are you working on, my love?" asked Mama, carrying a clean and freshly changed Ismail. She put him down to play with a set of blocks.

I grabbed an apple slice and gave it an angry crunch. "We're working on a project for social studies. Ammar and I are in a group with Jordyn."

"That's nice," said Mama. "Maybe she can come over and study with you, like Maryam used to." As soon as she said Maryam's name, Mama's lips tightened, and she looked down at the floor.

"It's okay, Mama," I said. "Maryam . . ." Before I could say more, the phone rang.

Mama grabbed it. "Hello."

"Yes, yes, this is Muna," she said, looking a little confused. "Who you?"

She paused and someone spoke on the other end. "Oh, Jordyn mother. Yes. Talk Noura," she said, and handed me the phone.

"Hello," I said.

"Hello, Noura, this is Jordyn's mom. I wanted to set up a time when I can come by to help your mother with her English lessons."

"Oh," I said. "That is very nice of you."

"It's no problem," she said, her voice friendly and warm. "It's something I'd told our church I'd like to do. When is a good time for me to stop by?"

"Hold on, please," I said. "I will ask my mother." I told Mama what she'd said.

"Oh my goodness, that is so generous of her," said Mama. "Well, she can come tomorrow afternoon for tea. Around one o'clock. I will make my cookies."

I nodded and shared what she'd said with Jordyn's mom.

"Jordyn told me about your mom's *kibbe*," she said, with a sad sigh. "I love trying new cuisines. You know, I used to take cooking classes at Sur La Table—Cajun, French, and Thai food."

I was confused. I didn't know what Cajun or Thai food was. I turned to Mama. "She likes all kinds of food and likes to learn cooking . . ." I frowned, feeling like I'd lost something in the translation.

"She wants to learn how to cook? That is wonderful," said Mama, a smile brightening her face. "Why doesn't she just come over for a cooking lesson? She is working so hard to help me. This way I will return the favor."

I turned back to the phone. "My mom would like for you to come for a cooking lesson," I said, wondering if that was something Jordyn's mom had been hinting at, or if I'd just gotten everything really confused.

"A cooking lesson?" Jordyn's mom said. "That's so generous of your mother to offer. I love hummus. And falafel. I'd enjoy learning to make food from Syria and the Middle East."

"Okay, then," I said. "Please come at one o'clock."

"Excellent, I'll put it on my calendar for tomorrow," she said, sounding super excited.

"Can you please bring Jordyn?" I asked. "We need to work on our social studies project."

"Absolutely," she replied. "I'm sure she'd love to come."

Feeling better, I hung up the phone. Mama was already running around, happily looking into the fridge to see if she had the ingredients for the menu tomorrow.

CHAPTER TEN

✣ JORDYN ✣

Saturday, February 18, 2017

After Saturday-morning swim practice, Mom and I drove toward the Alwans' apartment for our cooking lesson. I was relieved she had showered, blow-dried her hair, and put on lipstick. Except for the dark circles under her eyes, Mom looked normal.

"How was swim practice?" she asked.

I stared out the window as we crossed the bridge to Davis Island. "Lea swam faster than me, but it was okay."

"Speaking of Lea, you haven't invited her over in weeks," Mom said.

I shrugged. I hadn't invited Lea because there were no snacks in the pantry, and I didn't want her to see Mom walking around like a zombie.

A few minutes later, Mom shifted her SUV into park in front of the Alwans' apartment building. Before getting out, she opened her pocketbook and peered inside. "Ah, there they are. I made some English flash cards for Mrs. Alwan."

"How will she know what the words mean?"

"Google translate," Mom said. "She can write the Arabic word on the other side."

Though Mom had signed up to tutor Mrs. Alwan, I had expected her to back out because she'd been so depressed. The flash cards were a hopeful sign.

Mom took a deep breath, and then let it out. "Come on, Jordyn." I trailed behind as she climbed concrete steps with black metal railings to the second floor. I had forgotten there were no elevators and that the windows were so small.

Just as it started to rain, Mom knocked on the door of apartment 2F. Noura answered, and I almost didn't recognize her without a hijab. Her long, dark hair hung past her shoulders, reminding me of thick black velvet. "Welcome," she said. "Please come in."

Shoes were neatly stacked by the front door, and Mom and I took ours off too, even though I wondered why it was necessary. The Alwans' apartment looked much the same as the first time I'd seen it. The only real difference was a little boy lying on his stomach, watching *Thomas the Tank Engine*.

Noura spoke to him in Arabic and he waved at us. "Ismail doesn't speak much English yet," she explained.

"Hi, Ismail," I said. "Nice to meet you." I looked around the small apartment for Ammar. "Where's your brother?"

"He has a football—I mean soccer game," Noura said, "but will be back soon to work on our project."

Mrs. Alwan closed her bedroom door and glided toward us, wearing a long turquoise dress. She was elegant, petite with dark hair and aquamarine eyes. Clasping Mom's hand, she murmured, "Thank you." And then she turned toward me. "Noura and Ammar's good friend."

From the first moment I saw her, I liked Mrs. Alwan. She had a beautiful smile on her face as she served tea and cookies. "Eat, eat," she insisted.

Mom took a bite and said, "I've never had such delicious cookies. What do you call them?"

"*Maamoul,*" Noura answered. "Ismail saw dates in the grocery store and demanded Mama make them."

"I can understand why," Mom said, "and Ismail is adorable."

Mrs. Alwan's face glowed at Mom's compliments, and Mom seemed more like her old self. Maybe making flash cards and getting out of the condo had helped her forget her problems for a while.

After we finished our cookies, Mrs. Alwan headed into

the kitchen and we followed. As we passed the balcony, I was startled by the number of birds hovering around a feeder cleverly constructed from a milk carton.

Noura caught me staring. "Ammar built the feeder for me since he knows I love to watch birds."

"Wow, it's really awesome to have so many different kinds right outside your window."

"Yes, but I don't know all of their names yet. I'm still learning."

I was just about to tell Noura that watching fish had a soothing effect on me, and that I had an aquarium in my bedroom, when Mom called, "Jordyn, Mrs. Alwan's waiting."

Noura's mom had covered the kitchen table with a plastic cloth and stacked a pile of zucchini in the center.

Mom and I snuck glances at each other. I was out of my comfort zone, intrigued about what would happen next.

Noura set out bowls, knives, and sharp-tipped veggie peelers that she called *manakras*.

"We are making *kousa mahshi*," she said. "In Syria, we used a smaller squash called a *kousa*, but Mama cannot find them here, so we use zucchini."

Mrs. Alwan spread her hands. "*Kousa* short, fat." She cut both ends off a zucchini, then sliced it into pieces about four inches long.

Slicing was easy, but the next step took practice. Mrs. Alwan stuck the pointed edge of her vegetable peeler into the middle of a zucchini. She twisted and pulled out the core, in much the same way Dad would have opened a bottle of wine. Then she scraped the rest of the pulp into a bowl. "Now you try."

I was hopeless, but Mom was actually pretty good at coring zucchini. She had a big smile on her face, the kind I hadn't seen in a long time.

When all the zucchini were hollowed out, Mrs. Alwan mixed together hamburger, rice, and spices to stuff them.

I stuffed mine a little too full.

"Too much," Mrs. Alwan said. "It will . . ." She waved her hands.

"Explode," Noura finished.

Mrs. Alwan placed the stuffed zucchini into a pot of bubbling tomato broth that smelled like heaven—garlic, allspice, and meat. My stomach growled just from inhaling it.

Noura giggled. "It is good you are hungry, but the *mahshi* must simmer for a while."

Mom offered to wash dishes, but Mrs. Alwan wouldn't hear of it. "No, no," she said. "Sit, sit."

"Mama is right. You are our guests," Noura insisted.

Mom looked uncertain, but instead of arguing, she spread the flash cards across the kitchen table.

Mrs. Alwan clasped her hands together. "Mama is excited to learn," Noura said.

When the kitchen was clean, Mrs. Alwan took a seat beside Mom, and I followed Noura to her room.

She pointed to the floral quilt on her bed. "Thank you. It is most beautiful."

"You're welcome, but I'm the one who should be thanking you. My mom has been sad, and visiting with your mom is about the only thing that's cheered her up."

"Mama will be happy to hear that," Noura said. "She loves to cook and have friends visit."

"My mom used to be a good cook, but lately she hasn't made the effort."

"I understand. Mama used to write poetry, but she hasn't in a long time." Noura handed me a tablet and pencil from her desk. "You will have to instruct me. I have never done an American project before."

"Okay, no problem. We'll start by brainstorming."

Noura blinked, as if chewing over the words. "What does that mean?"

"It means to consider lots of ideas. Some kids will

probably paint posters; some might do PowerPoint presentations, or make dioramas, or build models."

Noura looked even more confused. Luckily, I had my phone and pulled up examples on the screen.

When I showed her a model city, Noura clapped her hands. "Ammar is a good builder," she said. "Come."

I followed her to the bedroom Ammar shared with Ismail. The walls were covered with drawings of an ancient city, and a small table held a 3-D model of a mosque, made from cardboard and painted paper.

"The Great Mosque was destroyed," Noura said. "Ammar was particularly fond of it—he loves architecture, and is building a model so we won't forget our home."

The pictures on the wall reminded me of the documentary we'd watched at church. I had had a bad dream about being trapped in one of the bombed buildings. And if I had had such an extreme reaction, I could only imagine how Noura and Ammar must feel. "What city?" I asked.

"Aleppo. Our home was in the city of Aleppo."

I used Google Images, and the before-and-after pictures of the mosque took my breath away. All that history ruined— gone forever. I sat down and studied Ammar's model. I wondered if building it was his way of coping with all the destruction he'd seen. "Noura, what if we wrote about the differences between an immigrant and a refugee?"

She didn't answer.

"Do you have another idea?"

She shook her head, so I continued with mine. "Immigrants leave their countries for better opportunities, but refugees don't have much choice. We could show before-and-after pictures of the mosque to illustrate that and put Ammar's model on display."

"I need to discuss this plan with my brother," Noura said. "Sometimes it is best to just forget." She stood and paced around the room. "But perhaps you are right. Perhaps we should be brave like Mohammad Qutaish."

"Who's that?"

"He is a Syrian boy famous for building a paper model of Aleppo. He is Ammar's inspiration."

I heard the apartment door close, and then loud footsteps barreling down the hall. Noura's eyes widened. "Maybe we shouldn't be in here," she said in a rush.

We were about to leave, but Ammar blocked the door, a frown pulling at his scar. "Noura, why have you brought a guest to my room?"

Ammar didn't raise his voice, but his fists were clenched.

Embarrassed, I held my palms up. "Sorry. I'll get out so Noura can explain."

As I walked down the hall, I heard them arguing. It made me really uncomfortable.

"Jordyn, you're just in time," Mom said. "The *mahshi* is ready."

As Mrs. Alwan ladled stuffed zucchini and tomato broth into bowls, Noura joined us in the kitchen. "Ammar wants to shower before eating," she said.

I hoped that was the real reason, and he wasn't still angry that I'd seen his artwork—a private part of himself that he hadn't been ready to share.

Noura took a seat across from me and tasted the *mahshi*. She spoke to her mom in Arabic, and then translated for us. "Thank you, Mama. As always, it is delicious."

"Mmmm, scrumptious," I said. I liked the open end best, where the rice was crunchy.

For a couple minutes, everyone focused on the yummy zucchini, but then Mom said to Noura, "Do you like to swim? Our condo has a pool."

Noura looked down at her bowl. "No."

I figured she'd never learned how, and the Alwans wouldn't have the extra money for lessons. "I could teach

you. During free swim at the aquatics center, there's a lifeguard on duty, so it'd be totally safe."

"No! No swimming!" Noura's voice was as sharp as the
manakras we'd used to core the zucchini.

I was stunned.

Mrs. Alwan admonished Noura in Arabic. The mood
around the table changed. No more smiles and friendly
chatter.

"I . . . I don't know what's wrong," I stammered, "but I'm
sorry."

Noura kept her head down. "Please eat. I'm sorry I
was rude."

We finished our meal in silence, except for Ismail. He
kept making train noises. "Chugga, chugga, choo, choo."

Noura's hand shook every time she raised her spoon.

Ismail whistled like a lonesome train.

"*Khalas*, enough!" Mrs. Alwan scolded.

Anxious feelings made the zucchini and tomato broth
churn inside my stomach. I wasn't sure what I'd done wrong,
but somehow, I'd offended both my friends. I looked over at
Mom. She was frowning, and the worry lines across her forehead were back.

CHAPTER ELEVEN

❧ NOURA ❧

Sunday, February 19, 2017

Lost. I was lost in a sea of iridescent aquamarine, deep navy, and sparkling turquoise with shards of glittering emerald and jade. The colors sucked me in, reflecting the sorrows and fears I'd seen swimming in Jordyn's eyes. I could feel the endless expanse of water beneath us, as it seemed our new home, Tampa, consisted of more water than land.

"Take deep breaths, Noura," Baba instructed, looking back at me from the middle seat of the minivan. "Start counting . . ."

My eyes remained glued to the endless water outside the car window.

"Is there no other route to the mosque?" asked Mama. She sat all the way up front, beside Amani, who was driving.

"Yes, but we can't turn around now," said Amani in a distressed voice. "There's no exit off the bridge. What's going on? Is everything okay?"

Noura, breathe. It's only water, I reminded myself as Mama explained in hushed tones . . . *water* . . . *frightened* . . . *her friend* . . .

I positioned my hands the way Dr. Barakat had taught me at the refugee camp in Kilis. Then I took a deep breath. *I'm flying. Flying like the beautiful pink bird I saw from the airplane window, flying over water.* Then I exhaled, and repeated.

"It's okay. Noura's got it under control," Ammar said, reaching between the seats to squeeze my hand.

I could see his worried gray eyes, so like Baba's, peering at me over the seat. I gave him a grateful smile as I breathed in and out, my heartbeat slowing, and my breath returning to normal.

"Family nights at the mosque are always popular," Amani said. "Imam Ibrahim insists we have them monthly." She steered into one of the last parking spots. "We're running late—it's nearly time for *maghrib* prayers."

Feeling a little light-headed from all that breathing, I climbed out of the car as the horizon faded into brilliant oranges and pinks. Ammar slowed to walk beside me as we followed the others across the parking lot.

He gave me a serious look. "You've worked really hard on Dr. Barakat's lessons, but you're still afraid. If you don't conquer your fears, they will conquer you."

I glared at him, annoyed at his sudden, superior attitude.

"You should let Jordyn teach you to swim," he continued.

"Jordyn probably wants nothing to do with us because you were so angry and mean about your model," I said. "She actually had a really good idea for our project, but you wouldn't even listen."

"You shouldn't have showed her my private things without permission," Ammar replied, in such a logical way it made me steam. "But you're right," he added with an embarrassed sigh. "I shouldn't have gotten so mad."

"Or been so rude," I added.

"Yes, that too," he mumbled. "But don't change the subject. Your learning to swim is different. It would help you become stronger. Maryam would have wanted you to."

Maryam? I squinted at him angrily. Though he had conquered the unimaginable and his face bore the mark to prove it, he had no right to pull Maryam into this. I opened my mouth to tell him just that, but suddenly his face lit up.

I followed his gaze past the trees at the end of the parking lot. The white-and-coral-colored mosque shimmered in the fading light. Illuminated by the golden light of dusk, it sat bedecked in graceful arches and angular lines. Two elegant minaret towers flanked each side of its facade. Ammar studied the structure with a builder's eye, following its gentle curves toward the copper dome that rested on top like a jeweled crown. I knew he appreciated how the architect had created harmony and balance. My brother's heart had always been in combining the science of construction with the art of design. He'd accompanied Baba and our uncles to the hotel's construction site and helped select tiles and woodwork for its interior.

Not wanting to mar his happiness, I bit my tongue and followed him through the great doors into the hall of the mosque. Immediately, a sense of peace fell over me. I took a deep breath and exhaled, letting the fear flow from my body. In straight lines, people stood along the red carpet, waiting for Imam Ibrahim to lead prayers. He was so tall and graceful in his brown felt robe and skullcap. His calm, welcoming smile brought me comfort.

"Noura, get in line," Mama said as Baba, Ammar, and Ismail headed toward the men's section. I noticed a lightness in Ammar's step, a sense of peace on his face.

I stood with my hands at my sides, waiting to begin, wishing we had a quiet, peaceful place to pray like this at school. A place where the other students didn't look at us like we were weird. Or worse.

~

All my life, I had only known Muslims who were from Syria. Of course, I knew Islam was practiced all over the world, but this was the first time I'd met Muslims from America, India, Sudan, Bosnia, Egypt, Indonesia, Afghanistan, and Mexico.

"Noura," Amani called as the men set up long tables for the potluck dinner in the banquet hall attached to the prayer hall. Women bustled around with steaming trays and dishes. "I want you to meet Lubna. I believe she goes to your school."

A girl with a chic, short haircut smiled at me. *"Salaam Alaikum,"* she said. "I'm in eighth grade; which grade are you in?"

"Walaikum Salaam," I replied. She looked familiar, with her tall, graceful build. "My brother and I are in the seventh grade."

"I'm sure it is all new and confusing for you, but you'll get used to it in no time," said Lubna encouragingly. "Do you have Mr. Fowler for social studies? I remember he takes being a good citizen very seriously."

I couldn't help but giggle. "Yes, he still does. And he reminds me of a bird, always pecking about, looking for answers as if they were seeds."

Lubna laughed. "You're right—that's a great description of

him! Well, if you have any questions or need help, you can always ask me, okay?"

"Yes, thank you so much," I said, feeling grateful that this grown-up girl was taking me seriously.

I looked around the mosque at all the families, the kids playing as if they didn't have a care in the world. And they didn't. There was no war here. There was no need to hide from bombs and guns, no starvation or disease. Baba stood talking with a group of men, and I caught snippets of their hushed conversation. President Assad had just hanged thousands of political prisoners. I shivered, thanking Allah no one we knew had suffered that fate. I spotted Ammar talking to a few boys. He looked as relaxed as the children, even carefree. Mama called me over and we got in line for dinner.

As I sat beside Ammar, I looked down at my plate, proud I'd taken samples of food I'd never tasted before. In addition to Mama's delicious *fatteh*—fried pita bread covered in chickpeas and yogurt—I'd chosen *mantu*, which were lamb dumplings; long noodles with shrimp and vegetables; barbecued mutton; *biryani* rice cooked with chicken and spices; and something called enchiladas with cheese inside.

"This is incredible," Baba said as he ate another heaping

forkful of *biryani*, the spices making him sweat. "It's spicy, but so good!"

"Here, Baba, try this," said Ammar, handing him a glass of mango *lassi*—a drink made of mango blended with yogurt and ice.

Mama smiled as she fed bits of bread to Ismail and chatted with a Bosnian lady in a long blue dress, whose blond hair shone in the chandelier light.

I was thrilled to see the happiness on Mama's face. Late the other night, I'd heard her crying after talking to her mother and sisters in Germany. The next morning, she'd appeared perfectly fine, hiding her sadness to make everything normal for us. But now, for this evening, Mama had found a sense of community, of belonging. And the people we'd met had been so kind, especially the woman from Lebanon who had offered to loan her some Arabic poetry books.

As I bit into a juicy dumpling, I thought back to the cooking lesson with Jordyn and how it had started out so well. The dumpling became dry and tasteless as guilt, which I'd shoved into the back of my mind, came flooding back. Ammar was right; I shouldn't have shown Jordyn his model. I should have told her about it, and then asked his permission to share it once he was home. Then we could have all brainstormed together.

Maybe that wasn't the only thing Ammar was right about. I swallowed the dry mouthful of lamb as regret settled over me. There was no way to hide that water frightened me, and that fear had made me snap at Jordyn, who'd only been trying to help. And it was that fear that kept me from being truly brave. Maryam, who would always be my best friend in the whole world, would not want that for me.

CHAPTER TWELVE

≈ JORDYN ≈

Wednesday, February 22, 2017

On Monday, Noura and Ammar avoided me at school. They avoided me on Tuesday too. So, on Wednesday, I decided not to even look at them. I was minding my own business, copying the quotes Mr. Fowler had written on the whiteboard, when Lea whispered, "Uh-oh. Nick's passing around another cartoon."

Nick's cartoons were legendary. They were funny, but in a mean way, like the one of Bailey's pimple exploding over the entire school. Last year, he'd drawn one of me so humiliating I'd wanted to disappear. Lea had urged me to tell on him, but a cartoon about my first bra wasn't something I wanted to show a teacher.

I copied another quote from the whiteboard, hoping Nick's latest creation had nothing to do with me: **The rule of law is more of an ideal we strive to achieve, but sometimes fail to live up to. www.americanbar.org.**

Before I had the chance to copy the next quote, Nick's cartoon landed on my desk. It showed a boy ripping off Noura's headscarf, and underneath, she was bald. Horrified, I stared at it, realizing I had three choices:

1. Pass it on. (Definitely not an option.)
2. Give it to Mr. Fowler and be labeled a snitch.
3. Slip it in my notebook and throw it away later.

I opted for number three and went back to copying quotes. **If men were angels, no government would be necessary. James Madison, Federalist Paper No. 51 (1788).**

Mr. Fowler finished writing and whistled to get our attention. "I'm going to give you a free period to work on your group projects. It's okay to rearrange desks, but I expect you to put them back at the end of class. And one last thing. Your homework is to research the history behind the quotes I wrote on the board."

I copied the last quote: **If I keep silent, nothing will change. Muzoon Almellehan, *The Globe and Mail*, December 5, 2016.** I'd never heard of Muzoon before, but her quote applied to my job as a student ambassador. Noura and Ammar were gonna have to talk to me, whether they liked it or not. I pulled my desk around so that we were sitting in a circle. Both of them looked away. Finally, I was ticked off. "If you don't want to be in my group, we can ask Mr. Fowler to reassign us."

Noura lifted her head, clutching the folds of her hijab. Her lips weren't turned down in a mad pout, but trembling. "It is not you," she whispered. "Ammar and I are ashamed of how we behaved during your visit. You were a guest and we made you feel uncomfortable."

Ammar cleared his throat and nodded.

"Really?" I shook my head, totally puzzled by her explanation.

"There were things I didn't want to talk about," Noura said, "things you do not understand. Terrible things that happened during the war."

I remembered the documentary from church again and felt sick to my stomach. It was hard for an American kid to imagine living in a city where bombs dropped nearly every day. "I'm sorry about what happened too. I didn't mean to upset you."

"We know," Noura said, "but sometimes it is difficult to make people understand that, though we escaped the war, we are still suffering from it."

Ammar fiddled with his pencil. "Noura said you wish to use one of my models."

I nodded. "Your mosque is beautiful. I bet we'd get an A."

"It is probably not good enough for such a high grade," he mumbled.

"It totally is."

A tiny smile snuck across his face.

I pushed ahead, hoping to convince him. "I could start with the poem that's in the Statue of Liberty Museum. That would satisfy the historical part. Then Noura could share the screening process for Syrian refugees. For the grand finale, you could talk about all the destruction in Syria and share your model."

Ammar's smile disappeared and his gray eyes darkened. "I don't know . . ."

Noura rubbed her fingers across her peacock brooch. "Ammar, you need to be one of the presenters. I know . . . I know it won't be easy. We could show pictures of how the mosque looked before and after the war, and tell them someday you want to help rebuild it."

Ammar's eyes narrowed into slits, and I knew it was time to stop pushing. "You totally don't have to. I mean, it's too personal, right?"

He frowned at me.

Noura tapped her index finger against the Muzoon quote she'd copied in bright red. "Don't let what happened in Syria take away your voice. You need to share your experiences *and* your talent."

Ammar's shoulders stiffened, and he spoke in Arabic. Noura glared at him. They argued back and forth.

"Hey, you guys need a referee," I said.

Ammar snorted, giving his sister one last angry glare. "Yes, we could surely use one."

I watched them, wondering again how Ammar had gotten his scar, and what he'd been like before the war. Had he been more outspoken? More easygoing?

The minute hand on the classroom clock moved. I silently counted to sixty, and it moved again. At this pace, we'd never get our project finished. "Uh . . . guys," I said. "We really need to figure this out."

Finally, Noura raised her chin and gave her brother a stern look. "You challenged me and I accept. Now you have to keep your end of the bargain."

Ammar's mouth flew open. I looked from one to the other, wondering what the challenge was.

"He told me he'd share his model," Noura said, "if I learned how to swim."

My mouth flew open to match Ammar's. After that day

in Noura's kitchen, I'd never imagined she'd let me teach her to swim. I still wanted to, but first, I needed to understand why she was so afraid. "Sure, that would be great," I said. "But . . . Noura, before we start, I need to talk to you in private. Could we have lunch together in the library?"

I bought a turkey sandwich in the cafeteria and met Noura in the library. We were all alone, except for our media specialist, Mrs. Warner. Noura had packed her lunch. A pita sandwich with thin-sliced lamb that she called a *shawarma*.

For the first few minutes, we ate our sandwiches without speaking, then Noura offered me some pastry. "I always thought baklava was Greek," I said.

Noura shrugged. "Syrians make baklava too."

She stared at me as I chewed, and I felt like a bug under a microscope—like she could see right through my skin and examine my bones.

In a serious voice, she asked, "Jordyn, why is your leg jumping?"

I pressed my hand against it to hold it still. "Because I'm afraid of saying the wrong thing, like on Saturday."

Noura shook her head. "That is not what I meant. When we were taking the exam, I saw that you were not doing too well . . . you were very anxious."

"I don't know what you're talking about."

"I know how it feels when it is hard to breathe, how your mind freezes and you want the earth to open up so you can disappear and hide."

I stared at her in disbelief. She knew! I buried my face in my hands. I didn't know what to say.

"I would like to exchange secrets," Noura proposed. "You tell me what is troubling you, and I will tell you why I am so frightened of swimming."

CHAPTER THIRTEEN

❧ NOURA ❧

Wednesday, February 22, 2017

I slipped Jordyn a napkin that Mama had tucked inside my lunch box. Without a word, she wiped her eyes, spent from sharing her secrets. From what she'd said, I could picture that terrible day at the swimming pool. A day that had been her best, and then her worst. She had lost her anchor—her feeling of safety and security. I sat beside her, trying to come up with the right words in English that would convey my sympathy.

I knew what it was to be unmoored, to feel like you had no control over your body and mind. I had seen horrible things during the war. Buildings blown up, cars demolished, entire city blocks reduced to rubble. And I'd seen people in despair, hungry, wounded . . . and worse. Never would I forget that hot summer, a few months after our apartment had been destroyed by mortar blasts. We'd been living in an abandoned grocery store when Baba got a text message. He'd grabbed his hard hat, prepared to join the other members of his White Helmet brigade. Since the city no longer had a functioning fire or police department, regular people like Baba—bakers, plumbers, engineers, and housewives—had formed the White Helmets to help those devastated by war.

When Baba realized I'd be left alone, he'd been forced to take me with him. Mama, who had been pregnant with Ismail, had gone with Ammar in search of bread, and there was no time to try to find them. We'd run through the winding streets until we reached what had once been a three-story apartment building. Baba and the other White Helmets had carefully combed through the rubble, gently extracting survivors who were covered in dust and blood. I'd been sitting in the safety of a broken-down car when Baba pulled a girl, a few years younger than me, from a deep hole. She hung limply in his arms, her face still, as if she were asleep. But when one of the rescued women gathered the girl to her chest and began to scream, I knew the worst had happened.

"Noura?"

Jordyn's voice pulled me away from Syria and back to the library. I shook my head to clear it of memories and said, "The loss of a baby is one of the most terrible things a family can suffer." I thought of Mama, pregnant with Ismail during the war. It had been a terrible time, but we had looked forward to welcoming a little brother or sister—a baby to bring joy and a spark of life. "It must be especially difficult for your mother."

"She's been really depressed," Jordyn said.

Then it dawned on me. Meeting Ismail had probably made it worse for Jordyn and her mother. They would never see their baby's first smile, or hear his or her first word. I felt anger simmer in my belly. "Have you ever questioned why it happened to you? Have you ever been angry at Allah . . . at God? How could he allow such a thing?"

Jordyn stared at me with eyes as blue as the sea. Slowly, she nodded.

I slumped in my chair, feeling the energy drain from me. "Me too," I muttered. "But I've learned that the world is not a fair place. Awful things can happen—like being caught in a war, or seeing everything you own vanish, or worst of all, watching those you love die."

"Are you okay?" Jordyn asked, squeezing my hand.

"Yes, but now I need to tell you my secret."

Jordyn gave me an encouraging smile.

"When we fled Aleppo, we left with another family—my best friend Maryam's. Our mothers had grown up together and were like sisters. We crossed the border into Turkey and ended up in the Kilis refugee camp. Then Baba and Maryam's father had an argument. Baba wanted to stay in the camp and apply to be a refugee. But Maryam's father was impatient. He wanted to get to Germany, like his older brother and Mama's family. To do that they would have to cross the Mediterranean Sea. Thousands of people were taking boats to islands in Greece, then making their way to mainland Europe."

I paused, remembering the night Maryam had come to our container, her emerald eyes shiny with excitement. She couldn't wait to get out of the boring refugee camp.

"What happened?" whispered Jordyn.

"They left the camp and made it across Turkey to Bodrum, a city on the coast." I swallowed, my throat dry. "Maryam's father called and said they'd paid a boat captain three thousand dollars to take them to Greece. He said they'd call as soon as they arrived. But we never got a call. A few months later, we found out their boat had capsized, drowning everyone on board."

"I'm so sorry," Jordyn said, her face pale under its tan. After a long pause, she whispered, "Is that why you're so afraid of swimming?"

I nodded. "Whenever I'm near water, I see Maryam disappearing into its depths." As the words left my mouth, I remembered my deal with Ammar. Before I could chicken out, I said, "I have decided to learn to swim."

Jordyn was quiet, considering my words. Then her eyes crinkled as she gave me a wide smile. "You're really brave."

I looked at her, feeling drained from reliving Maryam's death. "I don't feel brave at all."

"You survived a war, fled to a refugee camp, and made it all the way to America," Jordyn said. "That's pretty brave in my book."

I dredged up a smile. When she put it that way, it felt true. "But to get to here, I had a lot of help," I said. "When I first heard about what happened to Maryam, just looking at the small pond at the camp made me nearly faint. So, my parents took me to Dr. Barakat. She and a few other doctors had come from London to open a clinic. She was a psychiatrist—helping people whose minds were troubled from the war."

Jordyn nodded, encouraging me to go on.

"Dr. Barakat taught me how to manage my fear by using special breathing exercises. So now, when I see water, I'm still a little scared, but I don't panic like I used to. If I learn how to swim, maybe I can completely conquer my fear."

"I'm honored to help you," Jordyn said. "I promise to be a good teacher and to keep you safe."

I stared into Jordyn's dark blue eyes, weighing the truth of her words. I had heard many such promises in Syria. Another person cannot ever truly keep us safe, as much as they might wish to. Yet I could hear the sincerity in Jordyn's voice. This American girl had trusted me with her secrets, and I had trusted her with mine.

I smiled and nodded. "Okay," I said. "Teach me how to swim."

"It's a deal," Jordyn said. "Want to come to my next meet? It's Tuesday after school, and my parents could give you a ride."

"That sounds good," I said.

Jordyn stuck out her hand, and as we shook on it, I felt our bond strengthen. It is always good to face your troubles with a friend.

CHAPTER FOURTEEN

❧ JORDYN ❧

Friday, February 24, 2017

I dreamed about Maryam, a girl I didn't even know. I dove deep underneath the waves searching for her. It felt as if my lungs would explode, so I turned and swam toward the surface. As soon as my head rose above the murky water, I woke up with a shudder. The dream had been terrifying. I took more deep breaths, catching a whiff of pancakes. I hurried toward the kitchen, trying to put what had happened to Maryam out of my mind.

It was a relief to see Mom standing behind the griddle. She'd even poured the batter for my pancakes into cookie cutters shaped like fish—the way she used to do when I was little. A warm feeling washed over me. Safe. Unlike Maryam, I was safe.

"Happy weekend!" Dad said, with a big smile on his face.

I forced myself to smile back. Mom always used to make pancakes as a kickoff to the weekend, but hadn't in a while.

She'd had a couple sessions with a therapist, and her medica-
tion seemed to be working. From his seat at the kitchen
table, Dad eyed the pancakes, looking as hopeful as a little kid.

"Busy day?" Mom asked me.

"Just the usual. School and swim practice."

"My last appointment is at three thirty," Dad said. "I
should be home by five." He winked at me. "And I'd love to
take my two favorite girls out to dinner."

"How about Cuban?" I asked. "I could go for shrimp *sal-
teado* and key lime pie."

Mom flipped a couple of pancakes on a plate for Dad, and
said, "Cuban's fine by me."

"I'll make a reservation at the Columbia Restaurant in
Ybor," Dad said. "It's been a long time since we watched the
flamenco dancers."

While I was digging into my pancakes, Dad grabbed the
remote to catch the morning news.

A newscaster reminded boaters to report injured mana-
tees on their marine radios. "And now we have an update on
a breaking news story," he said. "Hillsborough County Fire
and Rescue has ruled an overnight fire at a Tampa mosque as
arson."

Mom gasped.

I stopped eating.

"Unbelievable," Dad said. "That's the second mosque fire in six months."

I hadn't paid much attention to the first fire, but because of Noura and Ammar, this one had my full attention. I remembered the beauty and symmetry of Ammar's model, and how the Great Mosque of Aleppo had been damaged too.

I listened as the newscaster talked about water damage from the sprinklers. The people who attended the mosque wouldn't have a place to pray for a while.

"Thank goodness the mosque was empty and nobody was hurt," Mom said. "That's one blessing."

"Yeah, you're right, but Mom, the Alwan family is probably afraid. They won't feel welcome in Tampa anymore. I wouldn't. Would you?"

"No, probably not," Mom said. She sighed and took a sip of her coffee. "But it's up to us to make them feel welcome. I'll call and set up another tutoring session with Muna."

"And I'll reach out to Mr. Alwan," Dad said. "I've been meaning to have my receptionist schedule appointments to get everyone's teeth cleaned, but it would probably mean more if I called myself."

I remembered having lunch with Noura in the library. I'd told her things I hadn't told anybody else, and she'd understood. But the worst part was thinking about Noura losing her best friend, only to move to the US and face prejudice here.

"Unbelievable," Dad repeated. "I thought we'd made more progress since the civil rights era, but I guess not."

We'd learned about the civil rights era at school—colored water fountains, signs that said, WHITES ONLY, angry mobs shouting at Ruby Bridges. I thought about Nick muttering *Immigrants are terrorists* on Noura and Ammar's first day at school.

"Normal people don't go around committing arson," Mom said. "Whoever set the fire must be mentally ill."

"Or maybe they've been radicalized," Dad said. "I recently read an article in the *Tampa Bay Times* that said the number of hate groups is on the rise."

"Hate groups?" I asked. "You mean like the Ku Klux Klan?"

Dad nodded.

I wasn't hungry anymore and pushed away my pancakes. I wondered what breakfast was like at the Alwans' apartment. They had to be angry and afraid too.

CHAPTER FIFTEEN

❧ NOURA ❧

Friday, February 24, 2017

Wearing my shimmering green hijab, I slipped my homework into my backpack and hurried to the kitchen. Ammar and I wanted to leave early so that we could do some research in the library before school started. From the hallway, I could hear Mama singing. It stopped me in my tracks. I hadn't heard her sing . . . well, since forever. I recognized the words. It was one of her favorite songs from the famous Lebanese singer Fairuz.

"Tell me, tell me about my country tell me,
O breeze passing by the tree facing me,
tell me a story about my family, a story about my house,
tell me a long story about my childhood neighbor . . ."

The song filled the small kitchen with warmth and happiness. I paused in the hallway and took it in: Mama frying eggs, using her spatula like a conductor used a baton. Ammar feeding Ismail bits of bread spread with soft cheese, while Ismail laughed and played peekaboo in his high chair. For a moment, I thought of Jordyn and of her little brother or sister that would never be . . . I shrugged off the uneasy feeling and caught sight of Baba. He stood at the kitchen counter, waggling his eyebrows, trying to catch my attention.

"*Habibti*, it's Friday," he said. "What should we do this fine evening to celebrate your marvelous exam results? Go out for ice cream?"

"Baba, it was just a quiz," I said, exasperated. "But of course I'd love to go for ice cream. Is that even a question?"

Baba laughed, knowing my love of anything sweet and frozen. "There is a little place by the hotel, run by a lovely Vietnamese family, the Trans. I see it whenever I ride my bike to work. I poked my head in the other day and saw that they have regular flavors but also mango, pineapple, and others I've never heard of—purple yam and green tea."

I hid a smile. Baba had already introduced himself and made friends with the Trans. It was so like him. I was just happy he was having breakfast with us. Usually he came home late, exhausted from lugging heavy bags for the hotel guests.

As I sat at the dining table, a sense of peace settled over me. For the first time since the war, it seemed everyone was happy, going about life as a normal family would—even Mama. Last night, she had reconnected with her favorite instructor, Professor Kahf, on social media. Mama had just begun her master's degree in Arabic poetry when the war started.

"Come," Mama called. "The bread is warm and the eggs are done."

As Ammar and I headed over, Baba's phone rang. He put his plate down and grabbed it. "Hello," he said. "*Salaam Alaikum*, Brother Jamal. How are you?" After a second, his smile disappeared.

Ammar and I paused, catching our father's stricken expression. *Something was wrong.* The warm mood of the morning cooled.

"No, of course, of course," said Baba. "Thank you for calling me. Now I know why you won't be picking me up from work." After another minute of nods and deep sighs, he hung up.

"What happened?" asked Mama, with a hot frying pan in her hand.

Baba's shoulders slumped. "Friday prayers have been canceled."

"*Why?*" asked Ammar, gripping his empty plate.

Baba rubbed his temples, a sign that he was getting a headache.

"Yes, *why*, Baba?" I chimed in.

"Someone set fire to the mosque," he said. "And painted on the outside wall . . . *Go Home.*"

"What?" cried Mama. "When? How?"

"Early this morning, before *fajr* prayers," said Baba. "Imam Ibrahim was notified and he rushed over to see what happened. Turns out the fire caused some exterior damage, but then the sprinkler system went off, damaging the interior of the mosque as well."

A memory of the sun shining from the mosque's copper dome returned to me. Of its tall pillars and prayer hall, filled with people praying in peace. My heart sank as the happiness of the room faded like a snowflake landing on warm skin.

Mama slumped down in a chair, looking distraught. "I thought we had left such things behind us. The violence and destruction . . . Who would do such a thing?"

"People who hate Muslims," said Ammar, his scar pinched from frowning. "People who hate us."

The smell of the frying eggs made me feel like I was going to be sick. But it wasn't the eggs, I knew; it was much more than that. *Go Home . . . But this was home now.* In one instant, the beautiful picture of what that morning had been was ripped into a thousand pieces.

CHAPTER SIXTEEN

⚘ JORDYN ⚘

Friday, February 24, 2017

Noura and Ammar were already in social studies class when I got there. They were both staring straight ahead and didn't acknowledge me when I sat down. Noura was wearing jeans and a pretty green hijab—a mix of an American girl and a Syrian one. I didn't know whether it was best to mention the mosque fire or pretend it hadn't happened. I wished I knew what would make it easier for them.

I sank down at my desk and checked the whiteboard. The Muzoon Almellehan quote was still there, along with some new ones. I'd done my homework and knew Muzoon was a Syrian teenager who'd lived in a refugee camp.

One of the new quotes was by Dr. Martin Luther King Jr. I copied it in my notebook: **The arc of the moral universe is long, but it bends toward justice.**

Mr. Fowler's eyebrows drooped as he perched on the edge of his desk. "Last night an arsonist set fire to one of our

Tampa mosques. To my Muslim students, I'd like to say I'm sorry, and that despite what happened, most Floridians respect your right to worship as you choose."

Joel raised his hand, which surprised me. He had barely participated in class since his mom got sick.

"Yes, Joel?" Mr. Fowler asked.

"I wanted to add that a couple days ago, somebody knocked over more than a hundred tombstones in a historic Jewish cemetery."

Mr. Fowler nodded. "It happened in St. Louis. I'm sorry about that as well."

Joel blinked his watery eyes. "You have to be a really awful person to tear up a graveyard." He glanced back at Noura and Ammar, then added, "Or set fire to a place of worship."

Mr. Fowler rose from his desk and walked over to the whiteboard. He tapped his index finger on one of the quotes and read it out loud. "'When I was a boy and I would see scary things in the news, my mother would say to me, Look for the helpers. You will always find people who are help-ing.' Fred Rogers."

As a restless silence settled over the room, Noura blurted out, "In Syria, my father was a helper. He was a White Helmet."

Everyone stared at Noura, and she slunk down in her seat as if she wanted to take the words back.

"Wow! That's impressive," Mr. Fowler said as his bushy eyebrows shot up. "I'll bet most of your classmates don't know about the White Helmet brigades. Would you like to tell them?"

Noura clutched her hijab, the way she often did when she was nervous. "Ammar, would that be okay with you?"

About a minute later, he spoke up instead. "After the war started and much of the city had been destroyed, no one collected the garbage; there was no electricity or running water. The police and firefighters had lost all authority, so ordinary citizens banded together. They wore white helmets and did whatever they could to help people.

"One day, I was with my father and uncle at our hotel. We were inside and didn't hear the helicopters at first. And when we did, it was too late."

I stared at Ammar as his words cast a spell over our classmates.

"The bombs fell, two or three, I think. The explosions tore through the building, but I don't remember a single thing. When I woke up the next day, I learned the White Helmets had pulled me from the wreckage. I'd cracked my jaw and was left with this," he said, pointing to the scar along his face. He looked around, as if daring anyone to speak.

Noura gazed at her brother with pride shining in her eyes. "Our father was so grateful to the White Helmets that he joined them. Once, I saw him dig among the ruins of a bombed building searching for survivors, just as other White Helmets had once searched for Ammar."

"You must be very proud of your dad," Mr. Fowler said, and then he stretched out his arms as if to hug the entire class. "Kids, be one of the helpers."

"I'm a member of the Save the Manatee Club," Penny said. "That's how I help."

I noticed Bailey's eyes were squeezed shut. I slipped her a note. **Bryan was a helper—a real hero**.

"In addition to looking for helpers," Mr. Fowler said, "in times of trouble, people look to great leaders. Whether it was FDR during the Great Depression, or Nelson Mandela during apartheid, a great leader sets the tone."

"A bad leader sets the tone too," Ammar said. "Assad is proof of that."

"Indeed, he is," Mr. Fowler said, and turned to switch on the classroom TV. "Let's see what our mayor, Bob Buckhorn, has to say about the mosque fire."

Mayor Bob was wearing a dark suit and a green tie. He stood behind several microphones from different news stations, flanked by Muslim men and women. He said a lot of important things, and Mr. Fowler scribbled one of them on the whiteboard. *Not on my watch, not in my city, we will not tolerate this.* When Noura and Ammar sat up straighter, I knew Mayor Buckhorn had set the right tone.

After the press conference, Mr. Fowler said, "There will be a solidarity gathering at the mosque tonight. I'm planning to be there. Mention it to your parents. Maybe some of you would like to attend too."

My parents and I had an early dinner at the Columbia Restaurant, then skipped the flamenco dancers and drove to the solidarity gathering. The sun was setting as we walked toward the mosque. Its dome and minarets reminded me of a building I'd always admired at the University of Tampa. The damage to the outside of the mosque was minimal, but Dad reminded me how the inside had water damage from the sprinkler system. Again I wondered who would do such a thing.

Mom covered her hair with a scarf and handed one to me. I slipped it on, but silently questioned if it was the right thing to do. I knew Mom was trying to be respectful, but I didn't want Noura to think I was pretending to be something I wasn't.

"A lot of people here," Dad whispered. "Probably a couple hundred."

I looked around at the news crews and reporters. Mom adjusted her scarf. "I heard there'll be a rabbi, a reverend, and an imam speaking."

Nearby, little kids were laughing on the mosque playground. I spotted Noura there, holding Ismail's hand. During lunch, I had told Noura and Ammar we had to talk, that it felt like there was an elephant in the room.

Noura had squinted at me with a confused look on her face. "Jordyn, why would you bring an elephant to school?"

I explained that having an elephant in the room is an expression my parents use. It means there's a subject everybody is thinking about, but afraid to mention.

"Oh," Noura said, and confessed the mosque fire had made her feel strange too. She'd said, "There is no right answer, Jordyn. I would have felt bad if you had ignored it. I feel bad discussing it—I just feel bad."

I looked around the large property for Mr. Fowler and saw him standing with Joel and his father. I followed Mom and

Dad to say hello to them, and then Mom pointed out Mr. and Mrs. Alwan. "Excuse me," Dad said. "It's high time I introduced myself."

Penny tapped me on the shoulder. "Should I have worn a headscarf?" she whispered, patting down her unruly hair.

I shrugged. "I have no idea. My mom handed me this one and I put it on, but don't worry about it. I bet it's more important to Noura and Ammar that you're here than what you're wearing."

Penny looked down at her green SAVE THE EARTH T-shirt. "I barely have any clean clothes. Mom's behind on the laundry."

My phone buzzed, and I pulled it out of my back pocket. Lea wasn't coming because her mom hadn't gotten home from work in time. I didn't ask about Bailey. I didn't think she would be comfortable attending.

As the service started, Noura walked over and stood between Penny and me. "Thank you for coming," she whispered.

The imam in a flowing white cloak spoke in Arabic, and then he translated the words into English. "I am thanking God for giving us this beautiful community who have come to us, reached out to us in solidarity and unity . . ."

A radiant smile lit up Noura's face, and she stretched out her hands, one toward Penny and the other toward me. It would have been much better if the fire had never happened, but since it had, at least we were all together, holding hands.

CHAPTER SEVENTEEN

❧ NOURA ❧

Tuesday, February 28, 2017

My nose wrinkled from the heavy smell of chlorine that lay over the indoor swimming arena like a thick blanket.

Jordyn's mom saw my expression and laughed as we took a seat on the bleachers overlooking the pool. "I've been inhaling that stink so long I can't even tell it's there anymore."

I looked away from the pool and returned her smile. "Are you feeling all right?" she asked, her eyes soft and gentle.

I knew Jordyn had told her about Maryam. *Of my fear of water.* "I'm okay," I answered.

"I think you're a brave girl to let Jordyn teach you to swim," she said. "I'm proud of both of you." She glanced over at Jordyn's dad, who was checking messages on his phone, and added in a quieter voice, "I'm so glad you came today. I know last week was incredibly difficult for you and your family. It's awful what happened to the mosque, but it's also wonderful to see the way the interfaith community have come together."

"Thank you for attending," I said, the memories of that evening flooding back. "My parents appreciated it very much."

"There's no need to thank me," she said, softly patting my shoulder.

I turned my attention to a group of girls, probably around eight years old, finishing their last lap. Jordyn's event was next, and she was still in the locker room. My eyes cautiously examined the cool aquamarine pool. *It's only water,* I thought. *I drink it every day and take a shower in it.* But the thought of being immersed in it sent a tendril of fear through me. I took a deep breath to steady my pulse.

I was reminded of how water had damaged the mosque even more than fire. It would be at least a month before it would reopen for services. My mind drifted to the thoughts that had been swirling inside me all weekend . . . of how strange it was that some people could be hateful toward Muslims, of how others could be compassionate, and that most fell somewhere in between. I wondered about the person who had been so full of hate that he or she had destroyed a place of worship.

I'd sat at Baba's laptop, donated by one of the families from the mosque, and looked up the Jewish cemetery in St.

Louis that Joel had mentioned in class. Someone had vandalized 154 grave markers at historic Chesed Shel Emeth.
Pictures revealed the terrible destruction—a line of knocked-
over stones inscribed with the names of those buried there.

But it wasn't just our mosque or Chesed Shel Emeth. The
news was full of similar stories. An African American church
had been set on fire in Greenville, Mississippi. And there
was more. A man with a gun had gone into a gurdwara, a
Sikh temple, in Oak Creek, Wisconsin, a few years back.
He'd taken six lives, destroying families and traumatizing an
entire community. And perhaps even worse, he was so stupid he thought Sikhs, a religious community from India
where the men wore turbans, were Muslims.

As I remembered the hundreds of people who'd gathered
at the mosque to show their support, I realized that both
hatred and compassion could reside in the same heart. In the
end, it was what you chose to do with them that mattered.

"Here they come," said Jordyn's mom excitedly, jarring me
from my heavy thoughts.

I watched the girls jog out of the locker room, flexing their
arms, full of energy. They wore caps, goggles, and sleek one-
piece bathing suits. I recognized Jordyn right away. She was

the tallest. As the others eagerly approached the starting
block, she slowed, hanging back. She waved her arms like she
was trying to shake something off. The girls climbed aboard
what was called a starting block—a square ledge where they
would dive into the water when their race started.

Leaning forward, Mrs. Johnson muttered, "What is she
doing?"

Jordyn stood for a moment, gazing out over the water,
until one of the other girls, Lea, I think, pulled her toward
her starting position. Jordyn shook her head, as if to clear it,
then stepped onto her block. As the girls bent down into
position, Jordyn remained standing. Her body began to
tremble.

Something is not right, I thought, a hint of concern weaving its
way from my brain into my heart. I remembered when Jordyn
had an attack of the nerves during our social studies exam.

Without warning, Jordyn crumpled, gasping for air.

Lea screamed and jumped off her block. "Coach B,
Coach B!"

"My baby," cried Mrs. Johnson, scrambling from the bleachers. In her haste, she left her purse as she ran toward Jordyn.

Mr. Johnson grabbed the purse and hurried behind her.
Unsure of what to do, I followed, my thoughts swirling like
a kaleidoscope.

By the time we got there, Lea had helped Jordyn to the ground.

Coach B was bending over her, holding her hand. "Jordyn, Jordyn, listen to me. You're going to be just fine, but I need you to breathe. Breathe, Jordyn, just breathe."

Mrs. Johnson sank to her knees. "What's wrong with her?" she sobbed.

"Try to stay calm," said Coach B, fumbling for her cell phone. "I'll call 9-1-1!"

Jordyn's dad knelt and hugged her mom. "Please hurry," he begged, his face as pale as fresh cream.

While Coach B described Jordyn's symptoms to the operator, Jordyn lay on the cold tile floor, gasping for breath. Instinctively, I sat near her head and took her chin in my hand. I spoke calmly, like Baba always did for me. "Jordyn, look at me."

She blinked, trying to focus. Her eyes met mine. "My heart," she gasped. "It's beating like a jackhammer."

I took her right hand and placed it on her chest, then her left on her stomach. "You are going to be okay," I said, keeping my gaze steady. "Now take a deep breath and fill your chest."

Jordyn shook her head, gulping, trying to drag in a breath.

"What is Noura doing?" muttered Bailey, crowding in behind me.

"Noura . . ." cried Jordyn's mom, but I ignored them all.

"I know you can do it," I said. "Pretend you are a bird, fly-ing high in the air, looking down. There is a cold, fresh breeze rushing over you. Now take a deep breath of that cold, refreshing air."

Jordyn grasped my hand and pressed down on her stom-ach as she dragged in a deep, ragged breath.

"Good," I said, so focused on Jordyn, it almost seemed as if I could breathe for her.

"The ambulance is on its way," said Coach B, running a hand through her short, spiky hair.

"Now breathe out," I instructed Jordyn.

As she kept breathing, in and out, I thanked Allah for the high-pitched wail of an approaching siren.

CHAPTER EIGHTEEN

❧ JORDYN ❧

Wednesday, March 1, 2017

I was terrified.

An oxygen mask,

IV,

ambulance ride,

EKG,

blood tests,

an overnight stay.

I suffered through it all, before being discharged from the hospital first thing Wednesday morning. All I wanted was to go home, take a long, hot shower, and sleep in my own bed. Instead, Mom drove me straight to her therapist's office, which didn't look like a therapist's office at all, but like a Florida bungalow, painted yellow with white trim. It even had a palm tree in the front yard.

Mom sat down in one of the rocking chairs on the front porch. "Sit," she said. "We're a few minutes early."

This part of Hyde Park had some quaint bungalows that had been converted into offices. I sat and watched traffic speed by.

"I think you'll really like Dr. Kelley," Mom said. "She's easy to talk to."

I shrugged, keeping my eyes on a driver in a red convertible, who'd slowed down and seemed to be lost. Lost—I knew what that felt like.

Mom reached over and patted my arm. "I wish you'd talk to me."

"I will, but not right now. I'm sort of nervous."

Mom checked the time on her phone and sighed. "Come on. We have to fill out new patient forms."

I was happy to complete the forms myself because it gave me something to do. Name, address, cell phone, birth date, Social Security number. I paused by the question that said, *Reason for today's visit.* I could have probably written an essay on that one, but since there wasn't a whole lot of space, I scribbled *panic attacks.*

After Mom turned in the forms to the receptionist, we made our way down a short hall to the second room on the right. The walls were painted a soothing mint green, and a comfy sofa and two chairs had been slipcovered in cream-colored denim.

Dr. Kelley rose from behind a sleek desk made of dark wood. She hugged Mom, and then shook my hand. "Jordyn, I'm Dr. Kelley."

Dr. Kelley looked like a model—long brown hair, a nice tan, and eyes the color of dark chocolate. I figured she was in her late thirties, like Mom. "Have a seat," she said, gesturing toward the sofa.

I sat down, leaning against a floral throw pillow. Mom sat beside me, and Dr. Kelley across from us in one of the over-stuffed chairs. "When I'm working with a young person," Dr. Kelley said, "I always start by talking to the family about confidentiality. Jordyn, what you say here is completely between us, but there are a couple of exceptions. One, if you were to say or show signs of harming yourself, or someone else, ethically I'd be required to speak up; and two, a judge has the right to subpoena your records, if there were any sort of legal proceedings."

I nodded. "Okay, but what about if one of my parents called you for an update?"

"I would refer them back to you." Dr. Kelley turned toward Mom. "I hope you understand that if Jordyn doesn't have privacy, she won't open up to me, and I won't be able to help her."

Mom tucked a loose strand of hair behind her ear. "Don't worry about us interfering. Jordyn's dad and I trust you."

Dr. Kelley smiled, revealing perfect teeth. "Great. Now that we've established the ground rules, I need to talk to Jordyn alone."

Mom squeezed my hand. "I'll be in the waiting room if you need me."

Dr. Kelley looked down and flipped through the papers on her clipboard. "The hospital faxed over your test results, and your heart is completely healthy."

I picked up the throw pillow and hugged it to my chest. "Yeah, but sometimes my heart doesn't *feel* healthy."

Dr. Kelley leaned toward me. "We're going to work on that. The more you tell me about your attacks, the better I can help you."

I took a deep breath and started from the beginning—the moment I dove into the pool a couple of months ago. Then I explained about the miscarriage, and how I hadn't swum well since. I told her about test anxiety, and how yesterday's attack had been epic—way worse than all the others combined.

Dr. Kelley nodded. "Wait. Let's talk about that. Did you have any added stress last week?"

"No, not really. I mean . . . I was a little worried about my new Muslim friends. After the mosque fire, I was afraid they wouldn't feel welcome in Tampa, and I thought a lot about my dad saying groups like the Ku Klux Klan are on the rise, but I don't think any of those things caused me to freak out."

"A panic attack is usually the culmination of a great deal of stress," Dr. Kelley said. "Worrying about the world we live in could certainly be a contributing factor, though. How are you feeling today?"

"A little nervous about being here."

Dr. Kelley looked up from her notes. "Most patients are. I can't make your anxiety go away, but I can teach you how to manage it. It's good your parents know about your attacks because support reduces stress. You might consider telling some of your closest friends and teammates too."

So far, I'd only told Noura, but after yesterday's meltdown, I'd have to tell my teammates something. I knew they'd all be whispering and wondering until I did.

Dr. Kelley gave me an encouraging smile. "Jordyn, you're not alone. About six million Americans experience panic disorder every year."

"Six *million*? That's a lot of people!"

"More than the entire population of Tampa," Dr. Kelley said.

I imagined all that anxiety hovering over the earth like a storm cloud. "What is everyone afraid of?" I asked.

"It varies. Some people are afraid to fly, or drive on expressways, or attend a crowded event—like a concert. Different people have different anxiety triggers."

"What about water?" I blurted out.

"Sure," Dr. Kelley said, "water could easily be an anxiety trigger for some people, but regardless of what triggers an attack, they all have the same physical cause—an imbalance of oxygen and carbon dioxide."

"Mom wanted me to mention that I'm teaching my friend Noura to swim."

"Oh," Dr. Kelley said. "I know about Noura. She's the daughter of the woman your mom tutors, right?"

"Yes, that's her. She's afraid of water because her best friend drowned fleeing Syria."

Dr. Kelley winced. "How tragic, but teaching Noura is an excellent idea. When you shift attention away from your own anxieties, your central nervous system releases positive endorphins. That's a fancy way of saying that helping Noura will make you feel better too." She paused and smiled. "Ready to get started? Learning proper breathing techniques should be really helpful for you."

When she said *breathing techniques*, I remembered the way Noura had rescued me. "I'm ready."

"The first technique is called square breathing. We'll breathe in for a count of four, and out for a count of four."

I slipped off my sandals, tucked my legs underneath me, and closed my eyes. Dr. Kelley spoke like a yoga teacher. "Breathe in, two, three, four. Breathe out, two, three, four."

I followed Dr. Kelley's voice, breathing in and out, picturing ocean waves lapping against soft sand. Every time my mind wandered, I brought it back to the beach.

After we finished, Dr. Kelley called Mom in and gave her a quick overview of our meeting. "Lori, your support is vital to Jordyn's progress," she said, and handed Mom a guided meditation CD. "You might try a nightly mother-daughter meditation practice. It would be good for both of you."

Mom looked down at the CD cover. She ran her index finger across it. "We'll start tonight. Jordyn's dad and I will do whatever it takes to help her get well."

"I appreciate your support," Dr. Kelley said.

Dr. Kelley looked away from Mom and over at me. "How are *you* feeling after our session?"

"Better," I said. "A tiny bit better."

CHAPTER NINETEEN

⚘ NOURA ⚘

Wednesday, March 1, 2017

In Jordyn's absence, Ammar and I had an appointment with the principal after school. "Do you think this is a good idea?" I whispered.

Ammar slouched beside me in the school office. "After what happened in the library, yes," he replied, his voice troubled.

I sighed. He was right. The library had been the last straw.

Since arriving at school, we'd tried to find a place for *dhuhr* prayers, and many times we'd missed them altogether. First, we'd tried a spot behind some leafy trees in the courtyard. It was a little uncomfortable since it was out in the open and we'd gotten strange looks and whispers. We had managed to deal with it, until Ammar got an empty soda can thrown at the back of his head. I had turned around to see who'd done it, and a group of kids lounged near the door. One was Nick, standing beside a tall, handsome boy with dark hair and a smirk on his face. A few girls stood with them, and they all pretended like nothing had happened. Then we'd moved inside, finding an unlocked classroom. But within a week, the elderly janitor, Mr. Lopez, found us. He'd stood politely as we'd finished up our prayers, but told us that we couldn't use the room again. Finally, we'd stumbled onto the perfect location—the stacks at the back of the library.

Ammar stood in one row, tucked between old encyclopedias, while I stood in the other, to his right. Today, I'd been in the middle of prayers, but I must admit my thoughts kept wandering to Jordyn: the way her face looked covered by an oxygen mask as she was loaded into the ambulance. Since our apartment was a block from the pool, her father had dropped me off at home before hurrying to the hospital. Mama and I had sat, drinking tea and worrying, until he'd called later last night and said that she was okay. I'd told Mama about Jordyn's episode before our social studies quiz. She had been surprised and saddened that we both suffered in the same way. It had been a year since I'd seen Dr. Barakat and although she'd helped me with my anxiety, it still lingered. I'd told Mama that I was fine, that I was going to conquer my fears by learning how to swim with Jordyn. At least, I hoped Jordyn would still be able to teach me . . .

As footsteps had approached, I'd tried to push thoughts of Jordyn away and focus on my prayers. I hadn't worried, thinking it was Mrs. Warner. She usually sat at the front desk and we felt safe, as if she were watching over us.

"Look, the terrorists are praying," muttered a deep, gruff voice. It was followed by a feminine giggle.

I froze, huddled on the floor. Three sets of shoes appeared beneath the stacks to my right. First there were sneakers, one set scuffed and black, a swoosh along its side. The second was smaller, dark purple high-tops with broken laces. The third pair was made from expensive leather.

"I want to know why they were allowed into the country. Weren't Muslims banned?" asked another boy.

Fear and anger surged through me as I tried to identify their voices.

"Shhh," whispered the girl. "The librarian will be back any minute."

"Oops," said the first boy, and without warning a stack of books came thudding down onto my back.

"Ow," I grunted, covering my head, more in shock than in pain.

"Noura, are you all right?" yelled Ammar.

I could hear him scrambling to get to me as the three sets

of sneakers took off. With Ammar's help, I'd pushed the books off, but by the time we ran to the front of the library, the trio had vanished.

So here we were, sitting in front of a large, organized desk that belonged to the principal, Mr. Thorpe. It turned out he was equally as large and organized as his desk, with a neatly trimmed brown beard.

"Hello, Noura, Ammar," said Mr. Thorpe with a smile. I noticed that his front tooth was crooked. "Thanks for coming in. I've had a chance to review the email from Mrs. Maisel. It's a request for a place to pray, correct?"

"Yes," I said, while Ammar nodded.

"We have been praying in different locations," I said in a rush. "And now we feel that it would be good to have a safe . . . peaceful place to pray. So we are not in anyone's way."

Mr. Thorpe looked over the silver rims of his reading glasses and frowned for a second. "Were you experiencing harassment from other students?"

"Harassment?" I said, my voice squeaking a little.

"No," said Ammar emphatically. "No harassment . . . no problems. We just need a more private spot."

I pressed my lips together, willing my tongue to stay silent. I had wanted to tell Mr. Thorpe the truth. That there was harassment . . . problems. But Ammar had been adamant. We couldn't say anything. If it got out we'd complained, things could get worse.

"Okay, I just wanted to be sure," said Mr. Thorpe, leaning back in his leather chair. "There is a district policy about release time. A student is allowed a certain amount of free time to follow a tenet of his or her faith."

"How does that work?" asked Ammar.

"It means that students can gather to pray as long as the same accommodations are made for students of other faiths," said Mr. Thorpe.

"That sounds fair," I said with growing excitement.

"I spoke with the staff about a suitable location, and it turns out there's an unused equipment room by the gym," Mr. Thorpe said. "Talk to Coach Stevens and he'll show it to you."

"Thank you!" Ammar and I said in unison, causing us all to laugh.

As we left the office, Ammar and I gave each other a relieved look. We had found a safe place to pray, a place that other students could use too, if they wanted. I couldn't wait to tell Jordyn.

CHAPTER TWENTY

❧ JORDYN ❧

Wednesday, March 1, 2017

After my appointment with Dr. Kelley, I took a long, hot shower, pulled on my favorite pajamas, and rummaged in the closet for Winnie the Pooh. I hadn't slept with Pooh in a long time, but hugging him made me feel safe.

When I woke up, Mom was sitting in a chair beside my bed, just watching me. She reached out and touched my cheek. "I love you so much," she said. "Anything that hurts you, hurts me."

This was *old Mom*, the one I'd been missing. "Don't worry. I'll be fine."

Mom nodded. "I know, but I've been so caught up in my own problems that I haven't paid enough attention to you, and that needs to change."

"It's okay, Mom."

She shook her head and said in a trembling voice, "No, it's

not, but I need you to forgive me, and I need to forgive myself too."

"Mom, you didn't do anything wrong." The guilt was creeping in again, threatening to smother me. "I'm the one who should be apologizing."

She frowned, and her forehead got those wavy worry lines across it. "Why in the world would *you* need to apologize?"

I squeezed my eyes shut, but tears leaked out anyway, and once I started crying, I couldn't stop.

Mom climbed in bed beside me, and held me as if I were a baby. "Shh," she whispered. "Shh. Everything will be okay."

I cried harder, big ugly tears, the ones I'd been holding inside for weeks.

"Tell me what's wrong," Mom said.

"I'm . . . I'm an awful person," I sobbed, "and I'm afraid you won't love me anymore."

Mom hugged me harder. "Jordyn, there is nothing in this world you could ever do that would make me stop loving you."

"B-b-b-but, it's my fault. I didn't really love the baby until after it was gone!"

Mom kept rocking me. "Oh, honey. Is that all? It's only normal to be afraid of change." She kissed the top of my head. "And it had been just the three of us for so long that a baby would have been a big change, but you'd have been a *great* big sister. As soon as you held the baby for the first time, you would have fallen in love."

"You really think so?"

"I know so," Mom said. She smoothed my hair behind my ear. "Looks like I'm not the only one who needs to forgive herself. Sometimes being human is the hardest thing of all."

When I woke up from my second nap, I was cuddling Pooh, and Mom was cuddling me. "We slept most of the day away," she said.

I reached for my phone from the nightstand beside my bed. "I want to send Coach a text and see if I can stop by."

"Why don't you wait until tomorrow?" Mom asked.

"Because I know my teammates are wondering what happened to me, and I'd rather tell them myself and get it over with."

"All right," Mom said, "you're right. The truth usually nips speculation in the bud."

Coach was staring out her office window, with the door open. "Coach?"

She turned, and a huge smile spread across her face. "Boy, it's good to see you standing there. You scared me half to death yesterday. But that girl, the one wearing the hijab, she was amazing!"

"Noura, her name's Noura, and she *is* amazing."

Coach sat down behind her desk. "Have a seat, Jordyn."

I leaned back in my chair and stared at the ceiling. I didn't know how to start, but Coach helped me out. "I know about your panic attacks. I called your mom at the hospital."

I kept staring at the ceiling. "I met with a therapist this morning."

"Jordyn, look at me," Coach said. "That's nothing to be ashamed of. If you'd broken a bone, we'd have called in an orthopedist; this is no different. You're seeing a doctor to get well."

Coach would probably never know how much what she'd said meant to me, and I couldn't think of words big enough to tell her. "I . . . I hadn't thought of it like that."

"It's absolutely true," she said. "Now, what do you want to do about your swimming? I'd recommend you keep practicing with the team, but put off competing until your therapist thinks you're ready."

I nodded, and my eyes brimmed with tears because taking a break felt like quitting, but I knew deep down I needed time to heal. "Coach, you know Noura, that girl you said was so amazing?"

"Yes."

"I'm going to teach her how to swim." I told Coach about Noura's fear of water and about Maryam.

Coach's eyes twinkled. "Jordyn, you have the heart of a champion. Let me know if I can help. When I teach you guys a new skill, I feel like a million bucks. I'll bet helping Noura will be like that for you."

I followed Coach to the locker room and took a deep breath before opening the door. "Jordyn!" the girls screamed. Lea and Bailey got to me first, pulling me into a hug, and then everyone else piled on.

They all talked at once. "Jordyn, are you okay? Can you still swim? You really scared us!"

Coach tweeted on her whistle. "Quiet, girls. Jordyn wants to explain what happened yesterday."

I started with Mom's miscarriage. All of the girls remembered when that happened, and then I told them about the anxiety I'd had ever since. I explained how it had gotten worse and worse, and that I'd been too embarrassed and ashamed to ask for help.

"I thought you were having a heart attack," Bailey said. "Like my grandpa."

"Me too," a couple of other girls chimed in.

"No, they checked my heart at the hospital. There's nothing wrong with it." I tapped my head. "It's all in here."

"*Chica*, I'm really sorry," Lea said.

Coach slung her arm around my shoulders. "How can your teammates best support you?" she asked. "Tell them what you need."

I shrugged. "I don't know exactly. Just keep acting normal and don't avoid me. Panic attacks aren't catching. I still need friends."

"She needs another group hug too," Coach said, and when they piled on for the second time, I closed my eyes and let their support soothe me, like the warm waves at Clearwater Beach.

CHAPTER TWENTY-ONE

❧ NOURA ❧

Friday, March 3, 2017

Ammar and I were beyond relieved to see Jordyn at school on Friday morning. I ran over to her locker and gave her a big hug. While we were catching up, Daksha stopped in the hallway to ask if she could help set up the new prayer room, then meet up later for lunch.

"Yes, of course," I said. "Mr. Thorpe said the room is for everybody to use."

"That's great," Daksha said, and hurried down the hall to catch Penny.

Jordyn frowned in confusion. "What prayer room?" she asked.

Ammar and I grinned and told her the whole story, and how news had spread. Lubna had found out about the prayer room from her mom, because Mama had told Amani, who then told her husband, and then he told Imam Ibrahim, so by the evening the whole mosque community was in the know. Lubna had called as soon as she found out and volunteered to help during lunch on Friday.

"I forgot to tell you something," Ammar said. "Mr. Lopez cleared out the broken chairs and old sports equipment after school yesterday."

My brother had already made a list of action items, started the moment we'd left Coach Stevens. Coach had happily shown us around the small, cluttered space and said that it was all ours, as long as we followed school rules.

I hid a smile as I looked at Ammar. It was as if he were leading an effort on a new construction site with Baba and his brothers. I hadn't seen him this happy in a while. He walked on ahead to catch up with a boy from his soccer team, and Jordyn and I stopped by the lockers.

"How are you?" I asked, though I'd already spoken to her on the phone the night before. She'd told me the doctors at the hospital had said her heart was fine, and there was nothing physically wrong with her, but she hadn't said anything else, and I didn't want to pry.

"I'm okay," she said, her hair falling over her face. "Kind of . . ."

"Kind of?" I prodded. In my heart, I knew she'd had a panic attack.

"My mom took me to see her therapist, Dr. Kelley," she said in a low voice.

"Therapist is like a psychiatrist?" I asked, remembering Dr. Barakat.

"Yes, I think so," Jordyn said. "I don't know the exact difference, but both deal with mental health problems."

"Don't be embarrassed," I said, seeing her reddened cheeks.

Jordyn pushed her hair out of her face. "Yeah," she said. "I ended up telling Coach B and my swim team about it. I guess the stress got to me, and I need help to get better."

"It could happen to anyone," I said, patting her on the arm as we headed off to class.

"Well, it isn't the Ritz," said Lea, with her hands on her rounded hips, as we all stood at the door of the small, dingy supply room.

"You can say that again," Bailey said, wrinkling her nose.

"But it's clean," Penny said, stepping inside, lugging sheets of brown and green construction paper, along with a basket of scissors and some tape.

"Yes," I said, "very clean. Mr. Lopez is wonderful." And he had been. He'd left the small room, about double the size of my bedroom at the apartment, spotless. But there was still peeling paint, and the small window would never be clear no matter how much Mr. Lopez scrubbed.

"It needs a rug," Lea said. "We have piles of them in the attic. I'll ask my dad for one."

"It smells musty in here," commented Lubna, tucking her hair behind her ear as she stood with one of her friends, a tiny girl with blue-streaked hair.

"Yup, a little like old feet," said Lubna's friend. "We need some incense, potpourri or something."

Penny and Ammar began drawing and cutting the shapes of trees from construction paper.

"What are you doing?" asked Lubna as she and her friend approached to help.

"We want to bring the outdoors in and create a tranquil space," Penny said. "In Japan, they have something called forest bathing. They conducted a huge study and found that being around trees improves mental and physical health."

"Cool," said Lubna as she and her friend started taping completed trees along one of the walls.

"Lea, Bailey, and I can make some flowers to go with the trees," Jordyn said.

"That would be great!" Penny said, with a huge smile on her face.

"We need more colored paper and pencils," Lea said.

While the girls took off to gather supplies, Daksha drew

henna-like designs for a border around the door. She was showing her designs to me when Mrs. Maisel walked in.

"How's everything going?" she asked.

"Great!" said Penny, and Ammar and I both nodded.

"Wow, you're really transforming the place," Mrs. Maisel said.

"Mr. Lopez cleaned it out for us," I added.

"Now, we're just making it feel a bit more . . ." Ammar waved his arms, and I knew he was searching for the proper word.

"Tranquil," said Penny, then explained the whole forest bathing thing to the guidance counselor.

"Well, as a reminder," Mrs. Maisel said, "the room is only to be used during lunch to practice tenets of your faith. The rules are very specific about that."

"Yes," said Ammar, with a serious look on his face. "We understand."

"And we appreciate that it was given to us," I added.

"The room is really shaping up," said Mrs. Maisel as she turned to leave. "And don't forget to eat lunch—you only have another fifteen minutes or so."

Feeling content and happy, I began to create the sign that would hang on the door. PRAYER AND MEDITATION SPACE. ALL ARE WELCOME.

CHAPTER TWENTY-TWO

 JORDYN

Saturday, March 4, 2017

Mom kept a whiteboard in our kitchen where she listed all our activities for the day. It had been blank for a while, but on Saturday it was full again:

1. 9:00: Jordyn swim practice
2. 10:30: Swim lesson w/Noura
3. 12:30: Ladies' luncheon!

The luncheon had been Mom's idea. She thought being around my friends would help ease my anxiety.

While I poured myself a bowl of Cheerios and sliced a banana on top, Mom got ready for the luncheon. She placed a vase of cheery tulips in the middle of the table and set out her good china.

"Are you sure the menu is okay?" Mom asked. "Muna is so

talented in the kitchen it's intimidating to cook for her daughter."

I shrugged. "Relax, Mom. The menu is fine." She'd decided to serve tomato bisque, two kinds of sandwiches—chicken salad and cucumber with cream cheese—fruit, gelato, and cookies.

As I finished my Cheerios, I watched the boats bob on the bay. "Mom, you should probably lower the blinds before Noura gets here. All that water really freaks her out."

"I'll remember," Mom said. "After Noura lost her best friend, it's no wonder living surrounded by water has brought back some bad memories."

In the locker room, Noura modeled her burkini. She looked cute, but it wasn't the kind of bathing suit I was used to. Noura's head was covered by a swim cap attached to a dress that stopped a couple inches above her knees, and her legs were hidden by loose tights, all in the same stretchy fabric. "Purple looks nice on you," I said.

Noura smoothed the skirt with her hands. "Thank you. Lubna has a cousin who outgrew it and gave it to me. The people we've met at the mosque have been very generous."

I stuffed my hair into a swim cap. "That's good. My cousin

used to give me hand-me-downs too. But now, even though she's two years older, I'm a head taller. Ready?"

Noura's eyes darted around the locker room, as if she were planning an escape from Alcatraz. It reminded me of what happened to Maryam. "Remember, there's a lifeguard on duty."

"It does not help to hear my life needs guarding," Noura said, her face more pale than usual.

I couldn't help but laugh. "Lifeguards are in case of an emergency, but we won't need one. We'll stay in the shallow end, and if anything makes you uncomfortable, you don't have to do it."

Noura sucked in her breath, and blew so hard she could have put out a hundred birthday candles. "I am ready," she said. "Lead the way."

I walked toward the pool at my normal pace—carrying a kickboard, with a beach ball balanced on top. Noura trailed behind.

"Jordyn, your legs are much longer than mine," she scolded, "and you walk too fast."

"Sorry about that." I put my stuff down and pointed out the lifeguard. "See, you're totally safe."

Noura trembled anyway, her eyes darting along the water's edge.

I sat on the side of the pool and patted the space beside me. "There's no rush. Have a seat."

Noura sat down, hugging her knees to her chest. She stared at the pool. "It is shallow compared to the Mediterranean Sea, but you can drown in a bucket of water."

"Where did you hear that?"

"I read it on the YMCA website. It said you can drown in any amount of water that covers your nose and mouth."

Smiling, I reached over and squeezed her hand. "The YMCA is right, but I promise to keep you safe."

"Have you always been so fearless around water?"

"Yeah, before Mom had her miscarriage, I swam like a shark." Reaching up, I clutched my coin necklace—a flying fish from the family Exocoetidae, and a souvenir of our trip to Barbados. "The water is still my favorite place to be, but I'm worried about competing. Afraid of that icky feeling when my heart speeds up and I can barely breathe. And the more I try *not* to think about the icky feeling, the stronger it gets."

"I know what you mean," Noura said, "but Ammar said we must control our fears, or they will control us."

"He's probably right." I slid off the edge of the pool into the water. "Look, it's only waist deep, and nothing like the ocean. You can see the bottom."

Eventually, Noura dangled her feet in.

I held out my hand.

She shook her head.

I decided to tell her a story. "Coach has me reading about other swimmers who have overcome huge setbacks. One of the best stories is about Yusra Mardini, who swam on the Refugee Olympic Team."

"Yes!" said Noura excitedly. "Yusra is from Syria like me. She was very brave, and when a boatful of refugees began to sink, she jumped into the water and pulled the boat to safety."

I pointed to the pool. "I need you to be brave like Yusra."

Noura's eyes grew soft and sad. "I am tired of always having to be brave," she said.

I searched for the right thing to say, but before I found it, Noura raised her chin and eased herself into the water. She shuddered. "I am not ready to put my face under," she said. "That would be too much like drowning."

"You know, learning to swim would make it far less likely that you'd ever drown. We'll practice kicking first." I held on to the edge of the pool and kicked my legs. Noura copied me. "Faster," I said.

Noura giggled and kicked as hard as she could. "Why did you bring the big ball with many colors?" she asked.

I reached for the ball and threw it to her. "For fun. To help you relax and get comfortable in the water."

When we were bored with the beach ball, I placed it on the side of the pool and showed Noura how to use the kickboard.

"No, I would rather stay by the edge of the pool."

I hugged the kickboard to my chest. "As long as you hold on, you won't sink, and if you get nervous, all you have to do is stand up. We're in the shallow end."

After some coaxing, Noura kicked her way across the pool, holding on to the board so tight her fingers turned the color of chalk.

I felt sorry for her and said, "Maybe that's enough for today."

Noura shook her head. "No, I accepted a challenge from Ammar. What is next, Jordyn?"

I showed her how to tread water. "Arms first. Just move your hands back and forth. Good. That's good. Now try kicking your feet and moving your arms at the same time."

"I am afraid to lift my feet," Noura said.

"I know, but think of it this way. You're taller than the water is deep. If you start to sink, all you have to do is stand up."

Noura lasted about two seconds. I clapped for her anyway. "That was good. Let's try it again and go for five seconds."

Her eyes grew wide and terrified. "I . . . I cannot. I see Maryam. I see her treading water. I see her growing too exhausted to move her arms and legs. And finally, I see her slipping beneath the waves!"

"Don't cry," I begged. "Please don't cry."

Noura sniffled, but couldn't stop the tears from flowing.

I put my arm around her shoulders. "Don't feel bad. We made progress today. Coach always says any progress is good."

Noura scrubbed her fists across her eyes. "Don't worry, Jordyn. I. Will. Not. Give. Up."

I nodded, thinking how it was possible to be both brave and terrified at the same time, and wondering if maybe that also applied to *my* swimming. Could I be brave enough to compete, while also terrified I'd have another attack? I really hoped so. I missed feeling free in the water more than anything.

CHAPTER TWENTY-THREE

✽ NOURA ✽

Saturday, March 4, 2017

It's amazing how hungry swimming makes you, I thought as I sat down at the table in the Johnsons' cozy dining room. Though I didn't think what I'd done in the pool was *actually* swimming, more like getting wet. But the way Jordyn had explained it to her mother and the girls, you'd think I was Yusra Mardini. Stomach rumbling, I took a sip of the creamy tomato soup followed by a big bite of chicken salad sandwich, studded with sliced grapes and pecans. Bailey plopped down beside Lea, balancing a bowl of soup and a plate piled with sandwiches.

"How's the chicken salad?" Mrs. Johnson asked as she placed a bowl of cut-up melon and strawberries in the center of the table. "I went to a halal grocery store and bought the meat. It was so nice to go to an actual butcher—at the grocery store, the meat's wrapped in plastic, and you have no idea where it actually comes from. The man behind the counter, Ali, I think his name was, gave me the freshest free-range chicken. I ended up buying lamb chops too, and nearly half a dozen bottles of spices so I can make some of the dishes your mother taught me."

"Thank you, it's delicious," I said, trying to smile through a mouthful of mayonnaise and chicken.

"What's halal?" asked Bailey, looking at her sandwich suspiciously.

Jordyn explained. "It's a process where the animal is killed after offering a religious blessing."

"Kind of like kosher for Jews," Lea added.

"Oh," Bailey said, and took a bite of her cucumber and cream cheese sandwich.

I pushed back my damp hair and happily slurped soup, catching Lea staring at me. Since Jordyn's dad wasn't home, I'd taken off my hijab to let my hair dry so it wouldn't turn into a soggy, knotted mess. Long and wavy, it flowed nearly all the way down my back.

"Don't worry, I won't steal your sandwich," I said with a smile.

Blushing, Lea answered, "Sorry, I didn't mean to stare, but I'm not used to seeing you without your hijab. Your hair is so long . . . and, well, beautiful."

"I don't know how you stand living in Florida with all

that hair stuffed under cloth," Bailey said. "Don't you
get hot?"

"A little, yes, but it helps keep the sun off my head too."

"Noura," said Mrs. Johnson, popping her head in from the
kitchen. "What time is your mom coming by for an English
lesson?"

"In half an hour," I said, glancing at the clock on the wall.
Mama was picking up English quickly and had started writing poetry again. She wanted to share some of her poems
with Jordyn's mother.

It was strange to wear shoes in the house, I thought, heading to
Jordyn's room. Lea entered first, while Bailey paused in the
hallway to retie the broken laces of her high-tops.

I passed through, pausing at the door to admire Jordyn's
beautiful white canopy bed. It had four posts hung with
sheer yellow curtains. There was a matching dressing table
and chest of drawers too. The walls were painted a rich
shade of blue and hung with posters of swimmers posing
with medals and trophies. There was an aquarium in the
corner with lots of bright tropical fishes.

"Wow, your room is so beautiful," I said, bittersweet
memories of our home flooding back. "My father's hotel had
beds like this made by artisan carpenters. They were

covered in velvet and the guests loved them—it was as if they were staying in a palace."

"Your father's hotel sounds amazing," Jordyn said as she and Lea each collapsed on the mattress. "Come join us."

I slipped off my sandals and climbed on the soft bed, and Lea sat up, her face troubled. "I can't even imagine how hard it must be for your father to lose everything. My dad lost his job last year and he was depressed for months, just sat on the couch and ate Doritos."

"It is very difficult," I said. "But we feel lucky to have escaped unharmed. Everything else we can rebuild."

"Except when someone dies," Bailey said, staring at her bracelet.

"That is the most difficult loss a family can suffer," I said quietly.

"Yeah," Jordyn said, hugging one of her stuffed animals. "Mom losing her baby is the hardest thing I've ever gone through."

"Or losing a friend," I said, thinking of bright green eyes that I saw for the last time in Turkey.

"Friend?" asked Lea.

"Yeah, Noura's friend . . ." Jordyn said, then quickly pressed her lips together, embarrassed.

"Friend?" asked Lea. "What friend?"

"Forget I said anything," said Jordyn, giving me an apologetic look.

Bailey's eyes narrowed. "Spill it. What are you guys talking about?"

I took a deep breath. "My best friend, Maryam, died when her family was trying to reach Greece from Turkey. They were all lost at sea when their boat sank."

"Oh my God," said Lea, clutching her throat. "That's awful. My *abuela*'s family escaped from Cuba on a boat, but luckily, it didn't sink."

Bailey looked pale and her hands shook. "I . . . I can't talk about this anymore."

Lea grabbed Jordyn's laptop from the side table and flipped it open. She asked Jordyn for the password, then went on the internet, hunting for music videos. Soon, lively upbeat music filled the room, lyrics belted out by a guy in leather pants with a guitar.

"Oh, this is a great song," said Lea, jumping off the bed to dance. "Come on, Jordyn, you need to let loose. You too, Bailey. Noura, come on!"

Grinning, Jordyn stood up and flapped her arms like a chicken. Bailey winced at the image, but Jordyn laughed and dragged her up to join them. Abruptly, the song changed—its beat familiar to my ears.

"I love this Shakira song," Lea cried, dancing in intricate steps and shaking her hips. "Come on, Noura, don't be shy."

Jordyn grabbed my hand and pulled me off the bed as the essence of the rhythm soaked through my skin and into my blood. In a deep, raspy voice, Shakira sang in Spanish and English, but the soul and cadence was from home. Half Lebanese and half Colombian, she mixed both cultures in her music.

I grinned, twirling around as the beat of the drums picked up, blending with the percussion. My hair flew as the girls danced around me . . . I closed my eyes and it felt as if I were with my Syrian friends watching *Arab Idol*. Soon, I was lost in the pulse of the music, its tempo taking me back home.

Exhausted and sweaty, we fell on the floor, all danced out.

"That was fun," Lea croaked, her voice hoarse from singing. "I think we needed to stop being so serious."

"Uh-huh," muttered Jordyn, splayed on the floor with her eyes closed.

Lea laughed, her dark eyeliner smudged. "I definitely needed it after working on our social studies project with Nick this morning. He is such a pain. An even bigger pain since he hangs out with my cousin Alexander. It would be okay if it was just at school, but he shows up to family parties too."

"Nick's not so bad," Bailey muttered. "When he saw a picture of Bryan in his dress uniform, he drew an awesome portrait for me. And Nick's dad . . . he's not an easy guy to live with. Nick, his mom, and his younger sister avoid him for the most part."

"Just because his dad is hateful doesn't mean he has to be too," Jordyn said. "He drew that awful picture of me wearing my first bra, and a cartoon of one of your pimples exploding over the entire school . . ."

"He drew one of Noura too," Lea said, and then gasped when Jordyn looked at her as if she'd lost her mind.

"What?" I asked. "What picture?"

Jordyn sat up, flushed, her hair falling over her face.

"Did you throw it away?" Lea asked.

"You didn't, did you?" Bailey said with a smirk.

"I want to see it," I said, my heart racing.

"I don't think that's such a good idea," Jordyn said.

"No," I said indignantly. "I want to see it."

With a tight face, Jordyn grabbed her backpack and pulled out a textbook. Inside was a folded piece of paper. Bailey snatched it from Jordyn's hand and smoothed it out.

I stared down at the picture and it hit me like a slap across the face. It was me. Without my hijab. And I was bald. I was horrified, both by his awful meanness and the fact that it was good. *Really good.* Without thinking, I snorted, then began to laugh in short fits.

Jordyn stared at me like I'd gone crazy.

Looking incredulous, Lea said, "I can't believe you're laughing."

"Why *are* you laughing?" Bailey asked, her eyes hard, almost angry as she stared at the picture.

I kept giggling, trying to talk, but couldn't. "He . . . he . . ." I said, then broke into gales of laughter.

Then Jordyn coughed, which turned into guffaws . . . Soon everyone was on the floor, laughing . . . until we were spent.

"Why the heck *were* you laughing?" Jordyn asked in an astonished voice.

I gave her a weak smile. "Nick would be so surprised . . . to find out I had all of this," I said, pointing to my head, "hidden under my hijab."

CHAPTER TWENTY-FOUR

✢ JORDYN ✢

Wednesday, March 8, 2017

After swim practice, Mom dropped me off at the Alwans' apartment to work on our social studies project. I left my shoes and backpack by the door and followed Noura into the kitchen. "Please have a seat," she said. "Mama has made *harisi*, and it's still warm from the oven."

I sat beside Noura and across from Ammar, who'd just lifted Ismail into his high chair. For a second, an image flashed through my mind of what our baby might have looked like. He or she would have probably been blond like me.

Mrs. Alwan served us sweet tea and slices of a golden-brown cake. I took my first bite, closing my eyes to savor it. "Mmmm, I love *harisi*. It has a nutty flavor."

"The nutty flavor is from tahini, a sesame paste," Noura said. "*Harisi* also has a rosewater syrup and some yogurt in the batter."

I wiped crumbs from my mouth with a napkin. "That's good to know. My mom will ask what we had for a snack. She's been googling Syrian recipes."

"She will have to come for another cooking lesson," Noura said, turning to her mom and speaking in Arabic.

Noura translated their conversation for me. "Mama said she would enjoy teaching your mother to make Syrian pastries."

I nodded enthusiastically. "That would be great! I know Mom would love it."

After we finished eating, Ammar offered to show me his model of the Great Mosque. I followed the twins to his room, relieved that he was taking the lead.

This time I could linger and really study the mosque. Ammar had built it using wooden blocks, cardboard, colored pencils, and glue. It had a large, rectangular courtyard, with a floor covered in geometric designs. "It must have taken you hours to draw the floor."

"Yes, it seemed like an eternity," Ammar said.

In the middle of the courtyard rose two fountains, both with domed roofs, and a slender tower with intricate designs and a balcony on top. "Ammar, this is spectacular! Forget an A. I think we'll get an A plus. Can I take a picture of it with my phone? I'd like to keep it."

"Of course," Ammar said, and pointed to the fountains with a proud smile on his face. "Those are for ablutions, cleansing before prayer," he said, nudging Noura with his elbow. "They work much better than the sink at school, eh?"

Noura rolled her eyes. "Just because you were born five minutes before me, there is no need to be a donkey."

I smiled at the joking around between Noura and Ammar. Sometimes watching them made me wish for a brother or sister. "While you two argue, I'll get my laptop. I can use my phone as a hot spot and connect it for research."

When I got back, Noura and Ammar were seated on the floor with their notebooks and pens. "Do you guys remember the poem I was telling you about? The one in the Statue of Liberty Museum?"

Both of them shook their heads.

"Well, I looked it up. It was written by Emma Lazarus. 'Give me your tired, your poor, your huddled masses yearning to breathe free . . .'"

"Those words . . . they touch your heart," Noura said.

I nodded. "Yeah, they really do, so I'd like to start our presentation with them."

"That is a very good idea," Ammar agreed. "Can you show me a picture of the statue?"

"Sure." I pulled up an image, and Ammar studied it closely.

"I am interested in the measurements of Lady Liberty, and the name of her designer," he said, "so I can read more about him."

"You can do that later," Noura scolded. "Don't get side-tracked. We have a project to complete."

Annoyed, Ammar swatted his hand in the air.

"Don't worry," I said. "When we finish, we'll look up the guy who designed the statue."

Noura impatiently tapped her pen against her notebook. "Jordyn, do not encourage him to rush through his work. We need to focus."

I hid a smile because Noura reminded me of a mother goose chasing her wayward goslings. "Well, since my part of the presentation is about the history of immigration, I thought Noura could share how it works today. That makes it more relatable, like reading about Anne Frank during the Holocaust."

Noura furiously scribbled in her notebook. "I think our classmates would be shocked by how difficult it is to immi-grate," she said. "I will interview Baba to be sure I understand the process."

"Perfect," I said, opening my laptop and pulling up images of the Great Mosque of Aleppo. "I'll flash before-and-after images on screen, while Ammar shows off his model and tells the class about how the mosque was damaged during the war."

"Since coming to America, I have not presented in front of a group," Ammar said.

"There is no backing out," Noura said. "I have already started swimming lessons. Now it is your turn."

Ammar rubbed his scar, and my eyes were drawn to it.

"How is my sister doing with her lessons?" he asked.

I remembered the way Noura had trembled in the pool during her first lesson, but had treaded water for thirty seconds during her next one. "She's very brave," I said.

Grinning mischievously, Ammar reached out and lightly thumped Noura's hand. "I am glad," he said. "My sister never backs down from a challenge, but I am the one who is always victorious!"

Noura pointed her index finger at him. "You are a donkey!"

Mrs. Alwan stuck her head in the door and spoke to them in Arabic. "What'd she say?" I asked.

"Mama told us to mind our manners," Noura said. "It is rude to argue in front of guests."

"Ah, that wasn't really arguing," I said. "Just kidding around the way Bailey and her brother, Bryan, used to. He called it *talking smack*."

"I didn't know Bailey had a brother," Noura said.

"Yeah, Bryan—his name is spelled out in beads on the bracelet Bailey wears. He used to be our swim coach before he joined the army."

"When you speak of Bryan, your eyes remind me of a storm cloud," Ammar said.

"Oh . . . I guess that's because he was killed in Afghanistan. Bryan was a great brother, and a great coach. Bailey was devastated."

Noura gasped. "I am so sorry to hear this. Everybody loses during a war."

Ammar nudged Noura with his shoulder. "It's better not to think too much about the past, but to be grateful we have a second chance."

I thought about what he'd said and jotted it down in my notebook. "That would make a great ending for our presentation," I said.

Ammar's eyebrows drew together, and he cocked his head to the side. "What do you mean?"

"Thanks to immigration, we have a second chance," I repeated. "*That* should be the theme to our presentation!"

CHAPTER TWENTY-FIVE

❧ NOURA ❧

Monday, March 13, 2017

With our social studies project almost complete, Ammar and I looked forward to our first service project. A service project was something the school did every year, but doing a coastal cleanup had been Penny's suggestion. The seventh- and eighth-grade classes had voted, and it edged out volunteering at the soup kitchen by ten votes. So, reporting for duty, I stood on the shoreline of Tampa Bay, looking out at mile after mile of crystal-blue water.

I saw the bay every single day from one vantage point or another, but this was the first time I had been close enough to get my toes wet. Now, as I probed the water's blue depths, my pulse was steady and my breathing even. I could skirt the shoreline and not feel as if I were drowning. I could even tread water or do the doggy paddle—thanks to Jordyn. But still, I kept my distance. No point in living dangerously.

I walked at the farthest edge of the group as we made our

way along the sandy shoreline. Both the seventh and eighth grades were participating so it was a pretty big group of kids, interspersed with teachers and chaperones. Up ahead, I caught a glimpse of red hair: Nick. An image of the drawing he'd made of me flashed in my mind, reigniting an ember of anger. *So much talent wasted on such a donkey.*

Beside him strode Alexander, who it turned out was Lea's cousin. He was an eighth grader and I remembered seeing him a few times—once in the courtyard when Ammar and I had been praying. With his curling dark hair and chocolate-brown eyes, he reminded me of Zakaria, a boy who had lived in our apartment complex in Aleppo. All the girls in the building had a crush on him. But unlike Zakaria, Alexander seemed to have an arrogance about him. Even though most kids were in shorts and T-shirts, he was wearing an expensive-looking button-down shirt rolled up to the elbows.

As one of the chaperones helped a girl whose shoe had gotten stuck in mud, Alexander and Nick elbowed a short, sandy-haired boy, trying to push him into the water. They would have succeeded, except Coach Stevens blew his whistle and called them over to him. When we passed by, Nick looked a little embarrassed, but Alexander stood with his arms crossed, staring at Coach Stevens with a smirk on his face.

"There he goes again," sighed Lea, who'd appeared behind me. "Alexander is always getting in trouble, especially when he's around Nick. But my aunt and uncle are so busy with their car dealership that they barely pay attention to what he's doing."

"Okay, everyone!" called Mark, a middle-aged man in khaki shorts and aviator sunglasses, who was the habitat restoration director. "We're going to stop right about here," he said, climbing on a small sand dune so we could all see him.

The mass of bodies slowed and shifted, finding spots around him. Ammar, who was usually close by, keeping an eye on me, was near the middle, talking to Joel. My heart constricted. Earlier this week, when Ammar had been late, we'd been running toward the prayer room. I'd found the door ajar and was about to burst through when I skidded to a stop. I held up my hand, silently telling Ammar to pause. A boy sat on the soft, paisley-patterned carpet Lea's father had donated. He'd been hunched over with his shoulders shaking and tears running down his face. It was Joel.

Concern shone in Ammar's eyes. "I'm going inside," he'd whispered. "The gym is empty. Quickly pray there."

Later, at home, he'd told me what had happened. He'd sat in the room after finishing his prayers, until Joel had turned to him. And without any prompting, Joel had told him that his mother had breast cancer and had just had a serious surgery. When Mama found out, she'd baked a batch of *maamoul* cookies and sent it to school with us for Joel and his family.

The habitat restoration director's voice pulled my attention back to him. "I'm so glad you could join us this afternoon," he said, in a booming voice. "We're going to spend the next two hours doing some trash cleanup, or marine debris, as we call it around here, which is a worldwide problem."

Penny stood in front, giving Mark her full attention as she and Daksha took notes.

"An estimated fourteen billion pounds of trash is dumped in the ocean every year," Mark continued. "It's not only ugly, but dangerous to marine life and human health. Since many forms of debris are nonbiodegradable, like plastic bottles, straws, and bags, they cause problems for years to come."

"Want to be partners?" asked Lea, handing me a bag and a pointy stick.

"Yes," I said. "Sorry, I wasn't paying attention toward the end."

"You didn't miss anything too complicated," Lea said, grinning. "Aim the pointy end of the stick at some trash, pick it up, and stick it in your bag."

I laughed. "I think I can do that." I took the stick and aimed at a plastic bottle. I missed, and it rolled away down a sandy slope. I hurried after it, cornering it near a bush. As I took aim again, I saw Jordyn and Bailey, standing together a few feet away.

"You don't spend time with us anymore," Bailey complained, her eyes shining with tears.

Surprised, I stopped. And without thinking, I slipped behind the bush.

"I don't mean to leave you out," Jordyn said. Her shoulders slumped. "It's just that I've gotten so busy working with Noura and Ammar on our social studies project and helping Noura learn how to swim. Plus, my mom has me going to all these sessions with her therapist."

"Noura and Ammar shouldn't take up all your time," grumbled Bailey. "What are you, their social worker?"

Social worker? Heat flared across my cheeks. I wondered whether Jordyn was pretending to be my friend because she felt sorry for me.

"C'mon, Bailey," Jordyn said. "You know it's not like that. They've had a really hard time. Coming as refugees, their mosque burning . . ."

"We've had a hard time too," Bailey shot back. "Bryan is dead because of these people . . ."

These people . . . I clenched the stick so hard it pinched the soft skin of my palm. How could Bailey think we had anything to do with her brother's death?

Jordyn's lips tightened. "Hey, that's not fair," she said. "I know you're still hurting about Bryan, and I miss him too, but . . ."

Bailey took a ragged breath. "I just want things to go back to the way they were . . ."

I didn't hear any more as they walked away, but I stood frozen behind the bush, my hand aching. The pain only added to the hurt and anger consuming me. I was tired of people blaming *all* Muslims for the terrible actions of only a few.

"Did you hear about the competition?" Penny called as she and Daksha hurried toward me.

Startled, I hid the anger in my face by bending down to pick up the bottle I'd been after.

"Yeah," said Daksha. "If you and your partner collect the most trash, you get a prize."

I smoothed my features and stood up, a fake smile plastered across my lips. "Really?" I asked, feigning enthusiasm.

"They're going to weigh our bags in an hour," Penny said, scurrying off as she found a couple of biscuit wrappers.

"Thanks," I said, and wandered off to look for Lea. The bright colors of the day had been diminished in my eyes. I looked over the now faded blue waters of the bay, back to the students, laughing, joking, and picking up trash together. Could people like Bailey ever change their minds and become true friends? I tried to rub away the pain in my palm, hoping with all my heart that Jordyn was not pretending to be my friend, just because she felt sorry for me.

CHAPTER TWENTY-SIX

⚘ JORDYN ⚘

Wednesday to Saturday, March 22–26, 2017

When I got home from swim practice, Mom was in the kitchen making chicken fajitas and intently watching the news. "How was practice?" she asked.

"It was pretty good. Coach has us doing some visualization exercises. We're supposed to close our eyes and picture ourselves swimming a perfect race."

"I think Coach talked to Dr. Kelley about how she can best support you," Mom said. She reached for the remote and, sighing, turned off the TV. "That's enough bad news for one day."

I leaned against the counter, searching Mom's face. "Why? What happened?"

Mom sliced open an avocado to make guacamole. "Nothing here in the US, but there was a terrorist attack in London at the Palace of Westminster."

"Was it a bomb?" I asked anxiously.

Mom shook her head. "A man ran his car into pedestrians on the Westminster Bridge. Several people are dead, and at least fifty people are injured."

"Was the man driving the car a Muslim?" I asked, thinking of what Bailey had said. *Bryan is dead because of these people.*

"Yes," Mom said, "but he could just as well have been a Christian. Dylann Roof, who killed African Americans in Charleston, was a member of a Lutheran church."

"Did the news anchors explain it that way?" I asked.

"No," Mom said. "Not really."

The fajitas didn't smell quite so yummy anymore. "Then kids like Bailey will hear the story and blame all Muslims, even Noura and Ammar."

"How are things going for them at school?" Mom asked. "Have they been treated unfairly?"

"Well, Nick has said a couple of things, but he's an equal-opportunity jerk. He's not very nice to anybody."

"You have to speak up," Mom said.

"I guess, but . . . I don't want Nick to bother me either." I'd never told Mom about Nick's cartoons, and I wasn't about to start now. She'd end up calling Mr. Fowler, and I'd have to relive the whole *Jordyn's first bra* incident.

"You look anxious," Mom said. "Why don't you lay out our yoga mats, and after dinner, we'll do a guided meditation?"

I went for the mats, but I wasn't sure how yoga could give me the courage to stand up to kids like Nick.

On Sunday afternoon, I sent Coach a text.

> **Me:** Swimming with Noura at 2:00 today. She's still afraid to put her face in the water.

> **Coach:** Want me to stop by?

> **Me:** That would be great!

Coach was waiting for Noura and me with a large plastic cup, a new pair of swim goggles, and a nose clip. "Hi, Noura," she said. "I'm happy to officially meet the girl who saved the day."

Noura shyly smiled. "I did not really save the day."

I remembered Noura's instructions. *Pretend you are a bird, flying high in the air, looking down. There is a cold, fresh breeze rushing over you. Now take a deep breath of that cold, refreshing air.*

Coach's voice brought me back to the present. "Hey, Jordyn, tell me about what you've taught Noura so far."

I told her about using the kickboard and treading water, but that Noura was terrified to put her face in, and I was worried about messing up and making her even more afraid.

"Why don't we all sit by the edge of the pool for a while?" Coach asked, lowering herself down, and then patting the tiles on either side of her.

Noura and I sat too, dangling our feet in the pool.

Coach took the plastic cup she'd brought, filled it with water, and poured it over her head.

"It's like taking a shower," I said, watching as Coach poured a second cup over her head. She handed the cup to me. "Jordyn, why don't you try it?"

I scooped a cupful of water and let it run down my face.

"Noura, will you give it a try?" Coach asked. "It's like Jordyn said, not much different than taking a shower."

Noura put a tiny bit of water in the cup, and then peered inside, as if it contained poison.

"You don't have to do it," Coach said. "You have complete control."

Noura closed her eyes, puckered her face, and splashed herself.

Coach grinned at me, while Noura sputtered and shook like a bird drying its feathers.

"Do you have any younger brothers or sisters?" Coach asked Noura.

"Yes, I have a little brother named Ismail," Noura said.

"When I teach toddlers to swim, I teach them to make balloon faces," Coach said. "Like this." She took a deep breath, held it for a couple of seconds, and then slowly blew the air out. "Now, you guys try it."

Giggling, Noura and I made funny balloon faces at each other.

"Jordyn, your cheeks look as round as an apple!" Noura said.

I sucked in my deepest breath yet and then released it. "I'm imitating a puffer fish!"

Coach slid from the side of the pool into the water. "Watch me. I'm going to take a balloon breath, keep my mouth closed, and get my chin wet."

After watching Coach and me get our chins wet, Noura did the same.

"The next step is a tiny bit harder," Coach said. "I want you to take a balloon breath, hold your nose closed with your thumb and index finger, close your eyes, and slide under the water."

"I am not ready."

"That's perfectly fine," Coach said. "I've seen it take kids as many as ten swim lessons before they were comfortable going underwater."

"You do not think I'm hopeless?" Noura asked.

"No," Coach said. "Not at all. What I want you to do is keep practicing every week with Jordyn until you're comfortable. After she teaches you to float facedown, I'll come back and work with you again."

"Wait," Noura said. She stood for a moment, closed her eyes, and took a deep breath. We gave her space. When she opened her eyes again, Noura looked more centered . . . more in control. "I am remembering Dr. Barakat's words. When I truly focus, I can accomplish anything." Noura quickly took a balloon breath, held her nose, and slid underwater!

When she surfaced, Coach and I were cheering, but Noura's bottom lip trembled. I didn't understand why until I noticed two eighth-grade girls, Carter and Maria, flicking water in each other's faces and shuddering the same way Noura had.

I stared at my shriveled toes, not wanting to cause trouble, but then I remembered what Mom had said. *Have they been treated unfairly? You have to speak up.* I hadn't stood up to Nick about the cartoon, but now I had a second chance. As we got out of the water, I whispered, "Coach, could I talk to you in private for a minute?"

"Sure."

We walked a couple steps away from Noura, wrapping

towels around ourselves, and I said in a low voice, "Carter and Maria are over there making fun of Noura, and I heard them whispering about her burkini in the locker room."

Coach's eyes narrowed as she turned to watch them.

I felt really bad for Noura. She had her arms crossed over her chest, like she was giving herself a hug.

Coach marched over and peered into Noura's eyes. "Will you trust me to take care of those girls? It's harder to mistreat people you know, and I'd like to introduce Carter and Maria to you."

Noura pressed her lips together and muttered so low I had to bend down to hear her. "It happens all the time." My eyes widened, but before I could ask her more, she turned to Coach. "Yes, I trust you."

After Coach walked away, Noura asked, "Jordyn, are you my friend just because you feel sorry for me?"

"What? No! Of course not. Why would you even think such a thing?"

Noura shivered and looked away. "I overheard you talking to Bailey at the coastal cleanup."

"Oh . . . I'm sorry about what Bailey said, but I told her she was wrong. Noura, look at me. I'm your friend because I like talking to you. You understand about my anxiety better than anyone. Remember how you taught me to breathe?"

A tiny smile snuck across Noura's face. "Yes, I remember. I played a small part in helping conquer your fear, and now, you will help conquer mine, by teaching me to float."

A few minutes later, Coach returned with Carter and Maria trailing behind her. "I think you girls know Jordyn, but I wanted to introduce you to our friend Noura. She's new here in Tampa. Noura, meet Carter and Maria."

Carter stared at her feet and mumbled, "It's nice to meet you."

Maria shook her dark hair into her eyes. "Yeah, nice to meet you."

"Since Noura is new here, she needs friends," Coach said. "I'm hoping I can count on the two of you to be among them."

I smiled, almost feeling sorry for Carter and Maria. I didn't think they would be making fun of Noura again any time soon, but I knew some kids wouldn't be so open-minded and nice, even after a lecture from Coach. As Noura said, it happens all the time.

CHAPTER TWENTY-SEVEN

❧ NOURA ❧

Wednesday, March 29, 2017

*B*e careful today. Baba's words echoed in my head as we hurried to school early that morning. I'd asked him why, but he'd just said that after the fire at the mosque and *other stuff going on,* it was good to be aware of our surroundings.

But Baba didn't have to spell it out for me. Lubna had told me earlier that week, a girl's hijab had been torn off by a group of boys at a bus stop. They'd harassed her and told her to *go back to her country.* Similar incidents around the US had caused many Muslims to wonder whether girls should stop wearing hijabs for a while. Mama and Baba had talked to Imam Ibrahim about it and gotten guidance that we should do what was best for our family. Though Mama and I decided to keep wearing our scarves, Baba and Ammar had shared a certain look I recognized well: *We must keep the family safe.*

Mr. Fowler had asked us to bring in our projects early so

that we'd be ready to present on Friday. So, I lugged a bag weighed down with sections of Ammar's project, while he carefully balanced his precious model. The mosque was light, but big and bulky, its minaret jutting up, making it awkward to carry. Ammar looked anxious, and I was a little worried about him. As the day of our presentation loomed closer, he grew more and more nervous. I'd helped him practice in front of the bathroom mirror, and when he relaxed, it was really, really good.

"Walk slower," grumbled Ammar. He lagged behind me on the sidewalk since he could barely see over the top of his model.

"Sorry," I said, slowing down. "Do you want some help?"

"Just tell me if I'm going to hit something," he said.

"Okay. We should be there in less than ten minutes. Not many kids will be at school this early in the morning."

As I walked along in the bright sunshine, a pair of pale gray pigeons swooped down over me, startled by a falcon flying overhead. One whirled low and grazed my hijab, setting it askew.

"You okay?" Ammar asked, laughing as he moved out of the way to avoid them.

"Hah!" I grumbled. "Even the birds have an opinion about my scarf."

That got a smile out of him and we walked on. But it got me wondering. *What would drive someone to harass a harmless girl wearing a hijab?* It would probably be the same type of person who'd set fire to a mosque or a church. Or worse . . . kill people. I sighed, the sunshine losing some of its brilliance. Perhaps it shouldn't amaze me so much. I'd seen such hatred and anger before, on the streets of Aleppo.

Neighbors and friends had turned on each other during the Syrian War. Of course, some of the tensions between the different groups—tribes, ethnic communities, Christians and Muslims—had always been there, but they were stoked into hatred by President Bashar and his father. They'd learned to keep power over the country by playing one group against the other. *Divide and conquer,* Baba called it. When you divide the unity and strength of a people, you can destroy them because they are too busy fighting one another.

I had thought America would be different. It was a country where immigrants had traveled from all over the world to become citizens, like Mr. Fowler said. But as we'd seen from the nightly news, there were tensions among the different racial groups and religious communities. The president had declared the Muslim ban and was building a wall to keep out other immigrants. There were protests where people carried signs declaring, BLACK LIVES MATTER. It bothered me that a group of people had to march on the street to demand that their very lives mattered. I sighed. Life was complex. After living through a civil war, I at least knew that much.

Up ahead, I could see the steps leading to the school. "We're nearly there," I called out to Ammar.

"Good," he grumbled. "My arms are killing me."

I glanced back at him to see how he was doing and spotted a sleek black Mercedes. As Ammar and I veered right, up the brick path that led to the steps and main entrance, it passed by us and stopped in front of the school.

"Ammar, the front steps are coming up," I instructed.

"Okay," he responded, peering around the model to gauge the distance.

I heard the car door open and then slam shut again, and a roar as the Mercedes drove off. I took one step at a time, keeping to Ammar's right so that I stayed out of his way. Footsteps approached from behind as we climbed.

Before I could tell Ammar to be careful, the boy leapt up the steps, two at a time. It was Alexander, Lea's cousin, and he had a smirk on his face.

"Be careful," I called out, irritated by the way he was crowding us.

Alexander frowned and gave me a cold stare. Instead of slowing or shifting away, he jumped on the step directly behind Ammar.

Confused, Ammar stopped, his model teetering in his hands. Alexander surged forward, his elbow ramming into Ammar's side.

"Oof," Ammar cried out, in surprise and pain.

I dropped my bag and tried to help him. But it was too late. The model slid from Ammar's hands. And like watching a movie in slow motion, it crashed onto the concrete steps with a sickening crunch. The front of the mosque smashed while the minaret snapped in two.

"Oh, *so sorry* about that," said Alexander with a laugh, then disappeared through the front door.

I didn't have the words that would put Ammar's model back together or make him feel better. So, I just sat with him in the prayer room, lunch forgotten since neither of us had much of an appetite.

After the *accident*, which had put Ammar in a fighting mood, we'd left the model, or what remained of it, on the table Mr. Fowler had set up for our presentations. Later, during social studies class, knowing looks had passed between the kids; the story was out about Alexander laughing at the *accident.* When I spotted Nick examining the ruined model, I thought I saw a pained look on his face. An artist viewing another's work. When Ammar had caught him staring, Nick had quickly averted his gaze.

As I sat in the quiet prayer room, memories tumbled back of our apartment in Aleppo before it had been destroyed. We'd huddled quietly in the dark, trying to listen to stories and poems Mama read to us by candlelight, blocking out the echoes of bombs, mortar, and gunfire in the distance. Shrugging off the old, best-forgotten thoughts, my eyes wandered across the small room, once again amazed at how much it had been transformed.

A row of cheerful paper flowers had been "planted" beside Penny's towering trees, their three-dimensional branches growing out of the wall, touching the ceiling. Many kids, some we didn't even know, had added all sorts of odds and ends: snowflake cutouts, cheery red-striped curtains over the window, and even soft cushions that you could use during meditation. Daksha had added a banner with the word COEXIST where the C was a Muslim crescent, the O a Hindu om, the E a combination of the male and female symbols, the X a Star of David, the I had a pentagram instead of a dot, the S a yin-yang symbol, and for the T, a Christian cross.

As we sat in the corner, a tall African American boy slipped inside, leaving his shoes at the door. He took a spot in front, facing the *qibla*, and started to pray. It was Malik, one of Lubna's classmates. He usually kept to himself, prayed, and left. But today he gave Ammar a fist bump and a nod before leaving.

"Hey," said Joel, appearing at Ammar's side. "I heard what happened. That really sucks."

Ammar nodded. Joel sat next to him, not making any conversation, just sitting in solidarity. Penny arrived. She stood next to the row of trees, closed her eyes, and raised her arms to the ceiling, where someone had hung a series of stars covered in foil. As usual, she stood while meditating. Other kids trickled in: Lubna and her blue-haired friend, Daksha and Lea. Some sat meditating; others read quietly, nestled against the cushions. Soon the room was filled with warmth, and a feeling of oneness settled over us.

Before I had the chance to miss her, Jordyn walked in and sat beside me, a look of sadness and confusion on her face. "I can't believe Alexander was such a jerk," she whispered.

I sighed. "I still can't figure out whether he pushed Ammar on purpose or whether it was an accident."

"Whether it was an accident or on purpose, Ammar's model was destroyed," she whispered. "What are we going to do about our project?"

"Don't worry," I said. "Ammar has a plan."

CHAPTER TWENTY-EIGHT

❧ JORDYN ❧

Friday, March 31, 2017

Presentations always made me nervous. I clutched my note cards with sweaty fingers and took a couple of deep breaths. I reminded myself of what Dr. Kelley had said in our last session—anxiety was normal and couldn't really hurt me.

"Do I have a group that wants to go first?" Mr. Fowler asked. He had set up a podium and a table with two chairs at the front of the room.

Bailey raised her hand. "Yep. I'll be the guinea pig. I'm ready to get this over with."

Nick groaned.

Lea said to him, "Suck it up, buttercup," and everyone laughed.

Bailey walked over and stood behind the podium, while Lea and Nick sat behind the table. "Our presentation is about the ocean voyages of immigrants," she said.

The first thing I noticed was that Bailey had memorized her speech and didn't need note cards. The second thing was that she couldn't seem to figure out what to do with her hands and kept playing with her bracelet.

"Steamships changed immigration," Bailey said. "Sailing across the Atlantic could take as long as six months, but the same trip could be made in only a week or two by steamship."

Nick, who was wearing a camouflage T-shirt, held up a large poster. He'd drawn a full-rigged sailing vessel and a steamship with a paddle wheel.

"Impressive," Mr. Fowler said, wiggling his eyebrows like a fuzzy caterpillar. "Nick, that is the most detailed drawing of a sailing ship I've ever seen from a student."

I grudgingly admired Nick's drawings. Any kid who'd ever seen one of his cartoons knew he had talent, but I was shocked when Mr. Fowler's compliment stained Nick's cheeks the color of a fresh raspberry.

As Lea took over from Nick, her hoop earrings swayed. "My family's immigration story started when Fidel Castro rose to power in Cuba," she said. "My *abuela*'s parents were so desperate to escape communism, they set out with their children in an overcrowded, poorly constructed boat for the US."

I had heard Lea's story before, but because of Noura's

friend Maryam, I listened to it in a new way. It didn't seem like ancient history anymore. I glanced over at Noura, and her eyes were puddled with tears.

When Lea finished, it was Joel, Penny, and Daksha's turn. They played a slideshow entitled *The History of Immigration Laws in the US.* "The Immigration Act of 1924 was passed to keep out families like mine," Joel said, pushing up his glasses. "It set quotas on immigrants from southern and eastern Europe."

Daksha joined in. "It also banned all immigrants from Asia, but then another law was passed in 1965 called the Immigration and Nationality Act, and that law gave preference to people with specialized skills. My grandfather came to the United States from Bengal, India, as an engineer."

I was interested in Daksha's presentation, but so nervous that I could hardly pay attention. And I didn't hear a word of Penny's speech because my heart was beating too fast. I closed my eyes and practiced square breathing the way Dr. Kelley had taught me, and pretty soon, I started to relax.

"Ready, group three?" Mr. Fowler asked.

I stood up, stumbled over my big feet, and almost face-planted on my way to the podium.

Nick laughed out loud and Mr. Fowler stared him down. "Apologize to Jordyn, immediately," he said.

"Sorry," Nick mumbled.

I placed my note cards on the podium and took a couple of shaky breaths. "The ti . . . title to our presentation is *Immigration Offers a Second Chance.*" My voice grew stronger. "The poet Emma Lazarus wrote these words in 1883: 'Give me your tired, your poor, your huddled masses yearning to breathe free . . . ' Those words are inscribed on a plaque that's in the Statue of Liberty Museum, but our country doesn't always live up to them." I used the example of the Chinese Exclusion Act of 1882. When Chinese immigrants were interrogated on Angel Island, those interrogations could last for months. "It took Noura's family over two years to be admitted to the United States. Now she'll tell you how immigration works today."

Noura passed me on her way to the podium and gazed out at our classmates. I could tell she was nervous by the way her hands trembled as she gripped her note cards. "Like Jordyn said, our family waited over two years to be admitted to the United States. After we fled to Turkey, we applied for refugee status with the United Nations." Noura looked down at her notes. "The formal name is United Nations High Commissioner for Refugees. UNHCR referred us for resettlement in America. It was not our first choice. Though we would have immigrated to any country—any country safe from bombs—Mama would have preferred to go to Germany. That's because we already had family living there. Immigration is a very frustrating and difficult process. My parents went through interviews, security screenings, finger-printing, medical exams, and more security screenings. We thought the process would never end. Ammar and I joked it took a thousand and one days." She paused and looked out at our classmates. "My parents have a dream to rebuild our lives, and for Ammar, Ismail, and me to get a good education and have a chance for success."

Mr. Fowler clapped. "Kids, think about what Noura just accomplished. She presented in English, which is not her native language. That's something most of us aren't equipped to do."

Noura looked down at the floor, but there was a big smile on her face.

Ammar carried his ruined model to the front of the room and set it on the table in front of him. A frown tugged at his scar, causing Noura and me to exchange worried looks. She'd told me he'd been practicing, and I crossed my fingers he wouldn't panic. I knew how humiliating that could be. Using one of the class computers, I showed a picture of the Great Mosque of Aleppo, with its square, blush-colored minaret covered in intricate designs.

"Construction on the Great Mosque started in the eighth century," Ammar said. He paused, as if doing mental math. "That means parts of it were built nearly a thousand years before America gained its independence. The photograph Jordyn is displaying was taken in 2012."

I flipped to a picture of the mosque a year later. Several kids gasped.

"The mosque has been heavily damaged in the civil war," Ammar said. He pointed to a pile of rubble. "This used to be a forty-five-meter minaret."

Penny raised her hand. "What exactly is a minaret?"

"A slender tower with a balcony. It is used by a muezzin, the man who calls people to prayers. It is similar to a bell tower in a Christian church."

Then I set our plan in motion. Using the picture I'd taken on my phone, I'd made a slide of the way Ammar's model had looked before it had been destroyed. I clicked on the slide, while he picked up the actual ruins. "My project is like the Great Mosque itself—damaged by hate."

Kids looked down, away, from side to side. Anywhere but at Ammar. Though Alexander had said what happened was an accident, most kids thought he'd tripped Ammar on purpose.

Ammar placed his model back on the table. "Jordyn spoke about the Statue of Liberty," he said, his voice growing more confident. "I have been researching her designer, the Frenchman Frédéric-Auguste Bartholdi. Do any of you know his inspiration for Lady Liberty?"

Daksha said, "She reminds me of a Greek goddess."

"That's a good guess," Ammar said, "but incorrect."

"Since the Statue of Liberty was a gift from France, maybe she's French," Joel said.

"Another good guess," Ammar said, "but wrong again. On a trip to Egypt, Bartholdi was inspired to design a statue he hoped would be placed at the entrance to the Suez Canal. But Bartholdi couldn't convince the Egyptian government to fund the project, and so he traveled to New York to convince the Americans they needed a statue, and when they said yes, the design of a Muslim woman became Lady Liberty."

"Bonus points!" Mr. Fowler crowed. "You unearthed a piece of history I didn't know about. Where did you find such an interesting tidbit, anyway?"

"Online at the Smithsonian," Ammar said, with a proud smile on his face. He checked his notes and continued. "One day I hope to return to Syria. Our country will need architects, builders, doctors, journalists. It will take many dedicated people to rebuild Syria." His voice shook. "This subject is personal to our family because thanks to immigration, *we* have a second chance."

I thought about all the immigration laws we'd discussed so far. Each one was personal and had affected real people, but it was easy to ignore laws passed by Congress until we heard the stories of real families who'd been affected by them. Noura and Ammar had their first birthday in America coming up, and I wanted to make it something special.

CHAPTER TWENTY-NINE

❧ NOURA ❧

Saturday, April 8, 2017

It was pretty simple. Jordyn had bribed me; not with money, but with the promise of birds. It was a little more complicated than that, of course. It had begun with two wrapped presents Jordyn had given us in the prayer room, coupled with a cheerful "Happy birthday!"

Ammar carefully tore into the bright red-and-yellow-striped wrapping paper, revealing a book called *World Architecture: The Masterworks*. He'd been dumbfounded and actually blushed, getting a laugh out of Jordyn and me. "It's marvelous," he'd whispered.

Inside my package was a book too: *Birds of Florida Field Guide*. "This is wonderful," I'd gasped. "How did you know it was our birthday?"

"It was on the paperwork my parents got when we decided to work with the church," Jordyn said.

I'd flipped open the pages and was staring at a stunning

pink bird, its eyes a bright yellow and its bill shaped like a spoon. *I had seen that same bird from the plane!*

"So," Jordyn had said, "do you want to see some of the beautiful birds in that book?"

"Yes," I'd said almost drunkenly. "Of course I want to see those birds."

And with that decision, I'd agreed to get on a boat.

"Are you *sure* you want to do this, *habibti*?" Baba whispered in my ear the following Saturday morning.

We were standing on the docks at Hula Bay Club, staring as an amazing contraption hoisted Mr. Johnson's sleek blue-and-white boat down from storage. It was like plucking a book off a shelf. Ammar was transfixed by the incredible mechanics of it as the boat was skillfully lowered into the water.

I straightened my shoulders, filled with steely resolve. Dr. Barakat's technique had never failed me, and I had grown more confident with swimming lessons. Surely, I could do this. I touched my peacock brooch, the only burst of color on my crisp white cotton shirt. Water would not turn me into a puddle of fear. "Yes," I said simply.

Mr. Johnson wore a blue cap over his sandy hair and gave me a warm smile. His teeth were just as Jordyn had described them in the letter she had left on my pillow: white enough to blind you. "I double-checked the forecast again this morning," he said. "No wind, water's smooth as glass—a perfect day for boating."

I nodded, still watching the ripples spread around the boat. "Mr. Johnson, I *am* a tiny bit nervous."

He gave me a warm, confident smile. "I've been boating all my life. Don't worry. I'll take it nice and easy."

"Thank you," Baba said, squeezing my shoulders.

Jordyn climbed on board and extended her hand to help me. "You can do this," she said as I lifted my leg over the side and clambered aboard. Clutching the railing, I took in my surroundings.

Mr. Johnson said the boat was a Robalo R200, and while that didn't mean much to me, I knew Ammar would be reading all about it later on the internet. In the middle of the boat rose a covered center console with a double seat. Jordyn's father sat behind the silver steering wheel, Baba beside him. There was additional seating in front of the console and behind it. I insisted on sitting behind, though Ammar looked longingly at the front. As soon as we were settled, Mr. Johnson expertly maneuvered the boat away from the dock, making his way around the other boats, both big and small, bobbing in the bay.

"Don't worry," Jordyn whispered, "Ammar and I are right beside you."

I crossed my arms over the life vest Jordyn had helped me put on as the boat picked up speed and the wind whipped my hijab. I closed my eyes. As long as I didn't look at the wide-open bay, it felt amazing—like flying over water!

A short while later, Mr. Johnson slowed the boat. He turned to look at us and said, "Are you ready for some fishing? We're nearly there, just another fifteen minutes or so."

"Yes, always ready," Baba said. "I used to fish with my father on the Euphrates River. Those are some of the happiest memories of my life in Syria," he added with a wistful smile.

"You and your family have been through a lot," said Mr. Johnson. "I really admire your guts and determination—it can't be easy to start over in a foreign country."

As Baba told Jordyn's father about his hotel, my thoughts drifted. Though I tried to rein it in, my mind went to Maryam . . . to the boat she'd been on as she'd left Turkey for Greece . . .

"You're incredibly brave for a girl," Ammar teased.

My eyes snapped open. He was annoying me on purpose, I could tell—to get my mind off my fears. I stuck my tongue out at him.

"Dude, I can't let that remark slide," Jordyn said with mock anger. "She's incredibly brave. *Period.*"

I reached into one of the insulated bags and pulled out my copy of *Birds of Florida Field Guide* as Jordyn and Ammar kept laughing and joking, trying to keep my mind away from all the water that surrounded us. When I looked at them, my heart was full. "You both helped me," I blurted out. "Ammar challenged me to conquer my fears and Jordyn helped me to grow more comfortable in the water. I won't become an Olympic swimmer, but I won't drown either."

Ammar laughed. "Yes, you're definitely not going to the Olympics."

"Hey," Jordyn said. "You never know. She's getting really good at doggy-paddling!"

Ammar snorted, and I laughed too. *Like that would ever happen.*

Jordyn bent down and reached into another insulated bag. She pulled out two leather pouches and handed one to Ammar.

"Nice," he said, reaching inside for a pair of binoculars.

"They'll help us find Noura's birds," Jordyn said, "and someday, I'd like to teach you guys to snorkel. Florida has some amazing fish too."

I set the guide on my lap and flipped it open, once again

amazed at how the book had been organized by the colors of birds. There was one section I'd pored over the night before. I wondered if I would see the bird I had first spotted from the plane when we'd arrived in Tampa. I had thought it was a pink flamingo, but it was actually a roseate spoonbill, a member of the Threskiornithidae family of birds. They had been driven nearly to extinction in the 1800s for their beautiful feathers, which were used to adorn ladies' hats. Slowly, the birds had made a comeback, but were still listed as a species of special concern.

Lost in my book, I didn't feel Ammar tugging on my arm. "Look," he said, handing me the binoculars. I stood and peered through them.

"We made it," Jordyn said, looking through the other pair. "We've reached Shell Key Preserve."

As my eyes adjusted, I saw the edge of an island, the bird sanctuary. There appeared to be hundreds of moving specks. As my sight cleared, I watched black-and-silver egrets feeding along the shoreline.

"Look at the blue ones," cried Jordyn, pointing to the right.

I turned my head and caught sight of fluffy powder-blue plumed birds, their featherless gray necks skimming the water.

"Here," said Ammar, having flipped to the blue section of the book. "They're called wood storks. Highly endangered."

"We'll go around the tip and anchor," said Mr. Johnson. "You guys can enjoy bird-watching while we fish. If you get hungry, there's water, soda, sandwiches, chips, and cookies. Just open the cooler and insulated bags until you find what you need."

"Thank you," we all muttered, but we weren't paying much attention to food. There were too many types of birds to see and identify.

As we turned a curve and wound deeper into the preserve, my heart flew to my throat. A sea of pink crystallized before me . . . a huge flock of roseate spoonbills settling in for mating season. I couldn't believe we'd found them! As I watched the birds, the shackles that had seemed to weigh me down fell away. I felt light enough to fly across the water, free to go wherever I pleased. Tears pooled along my lashes. The roseate spoonbills were home. Like me.

CHAPTER THIRTY

❧ JORDYN ❧

Thursday, April 13, 2017

As soon as swim practice was over, Mom whisked me away to Dr. Kelley's office. We got stuck in traffic and barely had time to catch our breaths before the receptionist called out, "Jordyn, Dr. Kelley is ready for you." I couldn't wait to tell her about my boat ride with Noura and Ammar.

Dr. Kelley greeted me with a big smile on her face. "So, tell me how you've been since our last session."

I kicked off my slides and tucked my feet underneath me on the sofa. "Good."

"Any panic attacks?"

"Nothing major, but I got nervous before I had to present in front of my social studies class."

"Then what happened?"

"I practiced square breathing the way you'd taught me, then my heart slowed down, and except for almost face-planting on my way to the podium, I made it through the presentation just fine."

Dr. Kelley clasped her hands together. "I'm so proud of you, Jordyn! Controlling your breathing was the best way to handle your glossophobia."

"My glossawhat?"

"Glossophobia. It's a fear of public speaking that's really common, but in my experience, the more public speaking you do, the easier it gets."

"Mom and I have been meditating too," I said. "Dad tried it once, but it put him to sleep."

Dr. Kelley laughed. "Keep up the meditation, and this week we'll add positive self-talk."

"Self-talk?"

"You've gone quiet on me," Dr. Kelley said. "What are you thinking about?"

"Handing out manna bags." I could tell by the confused look on her face that Dr. Kelley didn't know what I meant. "When you mentioned self-talk, I got this picture in my mind of a homeless man I see on the Tampa Riverwalk. He talks to himself. Sometimes Mom and I take him a ziplock bag with stuff like protein bars, sunscreen, and socks in it. Our church makes the bags, and we buy them for five dollars."

"That's a very worthwhile thing for you and your mom to

do," Dr. Kelley said, "but positive self-talk is a little different. Every time you have a negative thought, I want you to pause. Think about it for a second . . . and then turn it into a positive. For instance, *I'll probably have a panic attack at my next swim meet* becomes, *I'll probably be a little anxious at my next swim meet, but that's okay. I'll take some deep breaths and get through it.*"

"Something that easy actually works?"

Dr. Kelley leaned toward me. "It does. Some patients even carry around a small notebook. They write down their negative thoughts and reframe them into positive ones."

"You mean like, *I stink at oral reports* would become, *With enough practice, I'll get better at giving oral reports?*"

"Exactly," Dr. Kelley said.

"Okay, I'll give it a try. I'll even use a notebook. You know, Dad and I took Noura, Ammar, and Mr. Alwan on a boat trip to Shell Key. She was nervous about being surrounded by so much water, but ended up having a great time!"

"That sounds like fun," Dr. Kelley said.

I paused, wanting to ask my next question, but afraid of the answer. I pulled my hair around to the side and started braiding it. "Do you . . . do you think I'm ready to swim in competition again?"

Dr. Kelley stared at me for a long time. "What do you think?"

"I'm thinking . . . I'm thinking maybe I should skip the spring meets and shoot for the summer, or maybe even wait until fall."

"That sounds reasonable," Dr. Kelley said, "and it gives us a goal to work toward. If you'd like, I could attend your next meet."

"Is that allowed?"

She laughed. "Absolutely. I'd be there to support you, and we'd do some visualization beforehand. It's really nothing out of the ordinary. I've gone to a concert with a patient afraid of crowds, ridden an elevator with a claustrophobic, even taken a road trip with a woman afraid to drive."

I shook my head and imagined being on I-275, with cars whizzing by and a panicked driver. Now *that* was brave. "At least you won't have to do anything as drastic as swim in the lane beside me. Sure, I'd love for you to come."

"It's a date," Dr. Kelley said. "And, Jordyn, try and take the pressure off yourself. Being a happy, well-adjusted teen is much more important than holding a state record. I've spoken to your parents and your coach—they just want you to be happy."

I stared out the office window, thinking about happiness. I closed my eyes and tried to imagine my life without swimming. I thought about taking down the Missy Franklin and

Katie Ledecky posters from my bedroom walls. Of not swimming beside Lea. Of never again hearing Coach say, *Good job, Jordyn!* Thinking about giving up those things caused tears to leak from my eyes, and that's when I knew for sure I'd be back swimming my heart out. It was about freedom—about flying over water like the fish on my necklace. And when I remembered that free feeling, the one I *always* used to have, something inside me relaxed for the first time since Mom's miscarriage. Finally, I could breathe.

CHAPTER THIRTY-ONE

≈ NOURA ≈

Tuesday, April 18, 2017

Successful swimming lessons, a boat ride to see incredible birds, and now, Jordyn had had an amazing breakthrough with her counselor. It felt like things were looking up when I heard a faint, plaintive cry coming from somewhere down the hallway, near the eighth-grade wing.

I looked over at Ammar, confused. "Who *is* that?" I asked, but he shrugged.

The bell for lunch had rung a few minutes before, but we'd stayed to talk to the math teacher about an upcoming test. We needed to make *wudu* and quickly pray so we could have lunch with our friends in the courtyard. Penny had the idea to go to Disney World, and just the thought of meeting Mickey Mouse had caused my heart to beat faster. I hoped we could afford to go.

The strange wail came again, this time sounding as if it

was closer. It was followed by a garbled voice: "Ammar . . . Noura, where are you guys?"

"It sounds like a boy," I muttered as we rounded the corner and headed toward the bathrooms closest to the gym.

Before Ammar could push open the door to the boys' bathroom, a head popped out, followed by a plump body. It was Joel. His neatly pressed shirt and shorts were disheveled. He blinked, as if trying to focus behind his round metal frames.

"Thank goodness," he burst out, wringing his hands. "I've been looking everywhere for you guys."

"Joel, calm down," said Ammar, his voice as soft as when he was soothing Ismail. "What's wrong?"

Joel stood shaking, tears collecting in his eyes.

"Are you okay?" I asked, worry flooding through me. "Is your mom okay?"

"My mom? She's fine, better actually," he said distractedly, "but something terrible has happened," and he took off running.

Ammar gave me a confused look, but we started to run too.

"What's going on?" asked Lea, standing at her locker.

"I'm not sure, but Joel said it's terrible."

Lea slammed her locker shut and hurried after us. Joel

slipped past the eighth-grade wing toward the hall that led to the gym. I spotted Lubna and Malik talking near the water fountain, and when they saw us sprinting by, they followed. Malik's long legs sped past us, matching Ammar's strides.

Before Joel got to the gym, he slowed and slipped down a familiar side hallway, toward the supply room. He skidded to a halt at the open door, his hand gripping the frame. Ammar reached him first, and after looking inside, he turned, and the blood drained from his face. Malik froze and his mouth flew open.

I reached them next, and then Lea. What greeted me was utter destruction. I felt sick. The row of cheerful paper flowers had been uprooted and lay in balled-up scraps beside what had been Penny's towering trees. Their three-dimensional branches were scattered on the carpet, now littered with broken stars that had hung from the ceiling.

"What happened?" I whispered, stepping past the others to enter the prayer room. I skirted around the scattered cushions and shredded red-and-white curtains, noticing someone had dumped a ton of glitter onto the soft carpet. The once cheery snowflakes and posters with positive messages had all been ripped apart. Daksha's COEXIST banner had been torn in two and hung drunkenly by shards of tape.

Ammar stumbled into the room, followed by the others. He fell to his knees and clutched a cushion to his chest.

"All our work," said Lubna, choked up. "It's all gone."

I stood at the center of the room, feeling tears slip down my face. *Who hates us so much?* I thought. Although we'd been made to feel unwelcome before, this was the first time I had truly felt as if we would never belong. As if hate would win.

CHAPTER THIRTY-TWO

≥ JORDYN ≤

Wednesday, April 19, 2017

Our social studies class was silent. No papers rustled; nobody whispered or passed notes. I slouched in my seat, still numb from what had happened the day before. My eyes wandered to the whiteboard. As usual, Mr. Fowler had written one of his quotes. Normally, I would have copied it in my notebook, but I just wasn't motivated. I didn't think anybody was. Frowning, I let the words he'd written sink in.

Congress shall make no law respecting an establishment of religion, or prohibiting the free exercise thereof . . . First Amendment to the US Constitution

Prayer in Public Schools—The Supreme Court Weighs In:
Engel v. Vitale (1962)
Wallace v. Jaffree (1985)
Lee v. Weisman (1992)
Santa Fe v. Doe (2000)

I leaned forward and scowled at the quote. If we didn't live up to the principles our country was founded on, what was the point?

Mr. Fowler perched on the edge of his desk. His bushy eyebrows drooped as he examined our somber faces. With a sigh, he stood and paced in front of us. "Yesterday, several students stopped by to see me privately about what happened to the prayer room. Then, later in the evening, I heard from quite a few of your parents. I know some of you are sad, some are angry, and others just confused—wondering who did this terrible thing?"

I had thought about it almost nonstop. Who? Who had vandalized the prayer room? A list of names flashed through my mind. Was it Nick? He'd said *Immigrants are terrorists* and drew the mean cartoon of Noura. Or maybe it was Alexander? He'd tripped Ammar, and most kids thought he'd done it on purpose. One of the names left a sick feeling in my stomach, and I felt like a traitor for even considering it, but could it have been Bailey? She hadn't been the same since Bryan died, and when we did the coastal cleanup, she'd said, *Bryan is dead because of these people.* There was also the possibility it was a classmate I hadn't even considered. One who was angry on the inside, but hadn't shown it on the outside. Or maybe . . . maybe it was an adult?

I didn't wait my turn before blurting out, "I just want to know who did it, and I want them to be punished!"

Mr. Fowler looked at me with sadness in his eyes and paused before answering. "Jordyn, I understand, but you have to be patient and let the school conduct their investigation." He turned his palms toward the ceiling. "And . . . this may be hard to accept, but we may never know who vandalized the prayer room."

"This is true," Ammar muttered. "The police still haven't caught the person who set fire to the mosque, even with surveillance video."

Mr. Fowler pursed his lips, nodding at Ammar. "You're right. The police haven't made an arrest, at least not yet."

"Even though no one has been caught," Noura said, "something good has come from the fire. Someone at the mosque set up a LaunchGood account to repair the mosque, and he noticed that many of the gifts were in strange amounts . . . eighteen, thirty-six, seventy-two. And all the donors linked to the money had Jewish last names like Cohen, Avi, and Goldstein."

"They were giving chai," Joel said, a smile spreading across his pensive face. "It's a Jewish custom. When you give chai, you're wishing someone a long life."

"That's great," Mr. Fowler said. "It's wonderful to hear

that people across our community are stepping up to help. I call it feeding the good wolves."

"What do you mean?" Nick gruffly asked.

At the sound of his voice, Noura's shoulders twitched, and Nick slunk down in his seat.

"It's from a story called 'The Tale of Two Wolves,'" Mr. Fowler said. "Some people say it's a Cherokee legend, but nobody really knows for sure. It goes like this: One day, a grandfather was talking with his grandson. He said, 'Each person has two wolves inside him. The good wolf is brave and kind. The bad wolf is hateful and afraid. The wolves are always fighting.' The grandson asks, 'Which wolf wins?' The grandfather answers, 'The one you feed.'"

It was so quiet in the room you could have heard a feather fall. We didn't know who had set the fire, but we knew why . . . Hate.

CHAPTER THIRTY-THREE

❧ NOURA ❧

Wednesday, April 19, 2017

It was hard not to be angry. Or sad. Or disheartened. I looked across the dinner table at Mama and Baba and saw the same mixture of emotions flicker across their faces. Ammar slouched beside me, pushing a piece of kabob across his plate. It was always a troubling sign when my brother wouldn't eat, especially his favorite lamb kabobs drizzled with spicy tomato sauce. Only Ismail seemed happy, without a care in the world, sticking bits of cheese to his face. He was going through a white food phase and would only eat bread, cheese, milk, and rice. Mama just gave him what he wanted, hoping he'd get sick of them and eat something else.

"I think we should go back home," muttered Ammar, his eyes downcast.

Baba paused, chewing slowly, and swallowed before answering. "*Habibi*, we are home."

"No," said Ammar, dropping his fork onto his plate. The

sound startled Ismail and his eyes widened. "America is not home. We are not welcome here. The president made a ban against us the day we arrived. People stare at Mama and Noura just because they dress differently. They make fun of us when we pray. A person full of hate set fire to the mosque, and now another one has destroyed our prayer room."

Mama reached across the table and took Ammar's hand into her own. "I love Syria," she said, her eyes mournful. "I would like nothing more than to walk back into our apartment in Aleppo—visit my mother's house, go shopping in the souk, help my brothers at their bakery, or just stand and smell the jasmine while listening to the birds sing in your father's hotel."

Ammar bowed his head, tears running down his cheeks. I was stunned. He never cried. Not even when they'd pulled him out of the rubble, his face slashed and bloody.

"But, my love," continued Mama, "that life . . . that home is gone. There is no returning. We fought to keep it, but the price of our lives was too high."

I looked at my parents, the reality of what they . . . of what we had lost rushing back. I wanted us to be happy again. To be normal—at least as normal as it's possible to be after living through a war where we lost many family members and friends.

"As usual," Baba said, smiling gently at Mama, "your mother is right. To become a refugee, to leave the place of your birth, break with your culture and history, is like ripping away half of yourself. But we had to find a place where you, our children, would be safe and have a future."

"But America doesn't want us," said Ammar, angrily wiping his face.

I thought about what he said. Ammar was right. "I don't feel as if I belong either," I said. "So many people have hate in their hearts." Baba was about to speak, but I kept going, unable to stop the flowing words, because Ammar wasn't 100 percent correct. "But there are also others—Mr. Fowler calls them good wolves. Families, like Jordyn's, who have helped us. Students who came together and set up the prayer room. Even strangers gave money to repair the mosque."

"But it's not enough," said Ammar, the anger subsiding, leaving mostly sadness. "We have to always fight—to prove we are normal, that we are good people."

"Everyone has to struggle," I said, remembering Mr. Fowler's lessons on immigration and citizenship. "Except for the native people who lived here, or the poor Africans who were brought as slaves, everyone else came as refugees or immigrants. And most struggled—nearly each group had to face hate—the Irish, Italians, Poles, Jews, and others. After what happened in Syria, this is the place we need to build a home."

"Noura is right," said Baba, pride beaming from his eyes as he looked at me. "No place is perfect. There will be conflict wherever you are, but you have to find your . . . uh, good wolves, work hard, and live together in peace and harmony."

Ammar still looked disheartened, but he didn't disagree.

Ismail threw a piece of cheese at Mama, but she ignored it. Puzzled, she asked, "How do wolves have anything to do with this?"

"Uh, yes," chimed in Baba. "That confused me too."

Ammar and I looked at each other and started to laugh.

CHAPTER THIRTY-FOUR

❧ JORDYN ❧

Wednesday, May 3, 2017

We were running late! "Dad, can't you drive any faster?" I pleaded, anxiety pulling at me like a riptide.

Dad gestured with his free hand toward all the cars surrounding us. "Kennedy Boulevard is a parking lot. I'm doing the best I can."

"Close your eyes and take some deep breaths," Mom said. "We're cutting it close, but with a little bit of luck, we should get there before the meeting starts."

I leaned my head back against the seat, but instead of relaxing, I remembered all that had happened since the prayer room had been vandalized. Some parents were upset, calling the room a *mini mosque*. Other parents said there should be *no religion at all* in public schools. Still others wanted prayer in school, but only *Christian* ones.

Confused parents posted on the county school board whistleblower page. They sent angry emails and made phone calls. Pretty soon the school board stepped in and called a special meeting to discuss it.

Mr. Fowler had signed up online to speak at the meeting, and when he told us, Penny had asked if kids were allowed to weigh in.

"They sure are," Mr. Fowler said with a pleased smile. "Anybody interested?"

A lot of us had signed up, and now, while I was stuck in traffic, Lea, Daksha, Penny, Joel, Noura, and Ammar were probably waiting for me inside the Raymond O. Shelton School Administrative Center.

"You can open your eyes," Mom said, looking a little pale herself. "We made it!"

While Dad searched for parking, I watched people picket in front of the four-storied admin building. "Look!" I said, pointing to a man carrying a sign that said, BAN ISLAM.

"I don't have much patience for extremists," Dad muttered.

Mom grabbed my hand and we hurried past people clapping and chanting, "No religion in public schools! No religion in public schools!"

Things were calmer once we got inside. People whispered in small groups. I recognized Imam Ibrahim, chatting with the rabbi and the minister who'd spoken at the interfaith service.

"Good luck," Mom said. "Remember to breathe the way Dr. Kelley taught you."

I slipped down the aisle to the second row, joining Mr. Fowler and the kids from school. Noura gave me a weak smile, but Ammar didn't look up. He sat beside Joel with his hands crossed over his chest.

"Glad you made it," Mr. Fowler said. "I was getting worried."

"Sorry. Dad was running late because of a dental emergency."

I barely had time to scoot into the empty chair beside Lea before the school board members took their seats behind a raised platform shaped like a half circle. There was a podium with a microphone for those of us who'd signed up to address the board.

The chairperson, a serious-looking woman with short gray hair, called the meeting to order. Another member, Ms. Perez, announced a moment of silence, and then we stood for the Pledge of Allegiance.

Mr. Fowler had already explained to us how everything would work, but since I'd never attended a school board meeting before, I was nervous.

Superintendent Platt spoke first, leaning his wiry body toward the mike. "We've received a number of questions and complaints about the prayer room at Bayshore Middle School. As I began looking into the matter, I referenced a memorandum by the Florida Department of Education that's set to take effect on July first. This is a direct quote from the memo: 'The bill, which is called SB 436 Religious Expression in Public Schools, requires that students be allowed to pray or participate in religious activities or gatherings before, during, and after school, to the same extent secular activities or clubs are allowed.'"

The chairwoman said, "Thank you, Superintendent Platt. Our next speaker will be Brad Sawyer. Mr. Sawyer, you have two minutes."

Mr. Sawyer was a tall, red-haired man with a military crew cut. "That's Nick's dad," Lea whispered. "I met him when we were working on our social studies project."

"Is Nick here?" I whispered back.

Lea shook her head. "Bailey and Nick aren't coming. I heard them talking about it by the lockers."

"Bayshore Middle School is a secular institution paid for with taxpayer dollars," Mr. Sawyer said, in a booming voice. "It's not a mosque, or a church, or a temple. We stopped praying in public schools a long time ago, and I fail to see why we're making an exception for Muslims."

Noura sucked in her breath as he said *Muslims* in an angry tone. I wanted to tell her I was sorry, but the words clogged in my throat. We both watched as Mr. Sawyer went on to use up his entire two minutes ranting about the separation of church and state. He was the kind of man most people usually avoided—loud and angry. I actually felt sorry for Nick.

Mr. Fowler had told us the board members probably wouldn't comment or ask questions. That, instead, the chairwoman would call name after name from her list, until she got to the end of citizens who had signed up to speak. I watched the faces of the board members, wondering what they were thinking and how they might vote, but their faces remained neutral, and it was hard to tell.

The chairwoman called our principal, Mr. Thorpe, next. He spoke in a low, calm voice, as if he were trying to settle down a bunch of rowdy middle schoolers. He reiterated that Bayshore Middle School hadn't broken any state or federal laws, and that the room had been used by students of all faiths. He ended with "There was even a sign on the door that said, *Prayer and meditation space, all are welcome.*"

Next, the chairwoman called Imam Ibrahim. As he approached the podium, I could hear buzzing, like angry bees. The women behind me whispered about his long beard and brown cloak. Imam Ibrahim adjusted the microphone. "I would like to express our thanks to Mr. Thorpe," he said in a gentle voice, and paused for a few seconds before continuing. "Muslims have a requirement to pray five times a day, and one of our prayers, *dhuhr*, usually falls during lunch. We were very grateful to Bayshore Middle School for accommodating students who wished to practice their faith. I sincerely hope the improper actions of one individual will not infringe on the rights of many others. Thank you."

The chairwoman called Mr. Fowler. He was wearing a dark suit and strode confidently toward the microphone. He cleared his throat and began. "My name is James Fowler, and I teach seventh-grade social studies at Bayshore Middle School. Inside my classroom, there are Jewish students, Muslims, Hindus, Catholics, Methodists, Baptists, Lutherans, Episcopalians, and some students who don't practice any form of religion. The First Amendment protects the beliefs of all of them. It means Bayshore Middle School can't favor one religion over the other, or *hinder* any student from practicing the religion of his or her choice. The young men and women seated behind me are my students, and I'm proud they've decided to speak this evening. Thank you."

The chairwoman looked up. "Noura Alwan," she called.

Noura's eyes were wide, and her breath fast and shallow. I hoped she wouldn't faint.

CHAPTER THIRTY-FIVE

⮜ NOURA ⮞

Wednesday, May 3, 2017

N oura Alwan," called out the chairwoman, whose lips were puckered as if she'd eaten a sour lemon. I clenched the armrests with white knuckles.

"It's your turn to speak," said Ammar. He glanced at my face and frowned. "Are you okay?"

I took a deep, calming breath, and whispered, *"Bismillah-ir-Rahman-ir-Rahim, in the name of God the merciful and compassionate."*

"Noura Alwan?" repeated the sour-faced woman, peering into the crowd.

Ammar nudged me, so I rose and made my way to the podium. I faced the microphone while tucking in the edge of my bright-pink-and-cream hijab with a trembling hand. I'd chosen it because of its cheery, positive color and because it reminded me of the regal roseate spoonbills we'd seen from Mr. Johnson's boat.

I filled my lungs with air and began. "My brother and I met with our principal, Mr. Thorpe, and he said we could use a spare equipment room next to the gym for prayers. We'd been having a hard time finding a place to pray . . . and some kids had . . . some kids had not been kind when we were praying." Superintendent Platt frowned, which reminded me to stay calm and not mess things up. "But . . . but when our friends found out about the room, they all came to help us set it up. Penny created three-dimensional trees with construction paper. She hung them in the room and created a tranquil forest. Lea's family donated a beautiful rug. Daksha added a banner with the word COEXIST, where the C was a Muslim crescent, the O a Hindu om, the *E* a combination of the male and female symbols, the *X* a Star of David, the *I* with a pentagram dot, the *S* a yin-yang symbol, and for the *T*, a Christian cross. That is what the room became—a place for us to coexist, where we could come together and be ourselves." As soon as the last words left my mouth, I felt as buoyant as a balloon and floated back to my seat.

"That was amazing," Ammar said, his eyes bright, while Mr. Fowler beamed at us.

"Yeah," Jordyn said. "That was awesome."

"Thank you," I whispered, a feeling of freedom enveloping me. It was what Mr. Fowler had said in class: It was our responsibility as citizens to participate in the political system—to voice our thoughts and be heard.

"Joel Herzberg," the chairwoman called.

With a soft grunt, Joel got up from the other end of the aisle. He smoothed back his hair, combed neatly to the side, and wiped his hands on the side of his trousers. "Uh . . . hello, everyone," he said, pushing his glasses up on his nose. "My name is Joel Herzberg. I'm Jewish, and Rabbi Rosen from Beth Israel is here with my dad and me. This last year . . . this last year has been really . . . difficult." Joel paused a moment and blinked hard. "My mom was diagnosed with breast cancer. During the time she had surgery and was going through chemotherapy, it was nearly impossible for me to pay attention in class. My teachers tried to help, especially Mr. Fowler, but I just couldn't concentrate. Then the prayer room opened. It was a place I could sit quietly with my friend Ammar and pray for my mom. When all of us came together, it made me feel better." With a nod, and thanks, he trudged back to where his father sat.

The chairwoman called, "Daksha Patel."

"I'm the girl who designed the COEXIST banner," Daksha said in a rush, her small hands flying about like a pair of chocolate-brown finches. Then she paused for a moment and slowed down. "My family immigrated from India, and we are Hindus. There's only one other boy at Bayshore Middle School who's Hindu, and neither of us have felt like we truly belonged. A lot of kids used to ask us what Indian tribe we belonged to and pretend to be cowboys, shooting at us, like we were Native Americans in old movies. But when I'm in the prayer room, I don't feel different. I feel like I totally fit in, just the way I am."

When she slipped by me to get to her seat, I squeezed her hand. "That was really good," I whispered, my heart bursting with gratitude.

"It's true," she said with a sniff. "It's okay to be different. We have to accept each other the way we are."

"Penny Williams," the chairwoman called.

Penny stomped over to the podium and stood straight, wearing a T-shirt with a palm tree on the front. "I'm the girl who designed the trees in the prayer room," she said. "My family doesn't practice any sort of organized religion, but I use the prayer room for meditation. I like going there to think about nature and what I want to be when I grow up. And while I'm here, I want to protest the stupid new law that was passed, banning the ban of plastic straws." The chairwoman's brows shot up as Penny kept talking. "I mean, plastic is toxic for the environment. We were just doing a shore cleanup and saw the effects of plastic on wildlife." With that, she strode back to her seat.

"Uh, thank you for that," said the chairwoman, then called out, "Lea Rodriguez."

Lea's hoop earrings glowed in the overhead lighting as she confidently lounged against the podium. "I'm of Cuban descent and my relatives fled after the communists took over. My family's history is pretty common here in Florida and reminds me of what happened to my Syrian friend, Noura, who spoke earlier. In Cuba, the communists banned religious freedom. They even abolished Christmas Day. That's why freedom of religion is so important to me, and it's why I support the prayer room. For everyone."

As Lea sauntered back to her seat, the chairwoman called Jordyn's name. I looked at her as she took several deep breaths, in through her nose and out through her mouth. "You'll do great," I whispered, "you'll power through it like a shark."

With a last steadying breath, she gave me a wink and headed toward the podium. "I'm Jordyn Johnson, a United Methodist," she began. "Noura and Ammar are my friends, and I knew it was hard for them to find a place to pray. When I found out they got a room, I was really happy, but the room ended up not being just for them. I was diagnosed with an anxiety disorder. Being in stressful situations, like this one"—she paused, getting smiles from some of the board members—"gives me panic attacks. When the prayer room opened, it became a place where I could practice the deep breathing my therapist had taught me. I hope we'll be able to keep the prayer room because it makes everyone's day better. Thank you."

"Thank you, Jordyn," said Superintendent Platt. "I'd like to commend Mr. Fowler and his students. They are a testament to our strong public school system here in Hillsborough County. I know emotions are running high, so I'd suggest the board delay a vote on the prayer room until our next regularly scheduled meeting on May seventeenth."

"Delay?" I whispered to Mr. Fowler and the others. "Why the delay?"

"That means they're passing the buck," Penny said disgustedly as a grumbling roar filled the auditorium.

"Pass the buck?" I asked, confusion flooding through me. "What buck?"

"It means they don't want to make a decision right now and will vote on it later," said Mr. Fowler with a resigned expression on his face.

"Ah, c'mon!" Mr. Sawyer yelled as he stood up. "That's ridiculous!"

"Mr. Sawyer," said the chairwoman with a stern look, "I understand you're upset, but please take your seat."

"You don't know the meaning of upset, lady," shouted Mr. Sawyer, shaking his fist as his face turned as red as his hair.

"That's enough!" yelled the chairwoman as the other board members scrambled from their seats.

Mr. Sawyer marched down the aisle toward us.

I slid from my chair and crouched on the floor. "Noura," Ammar cried, coming to kneel beside me.

I tried to breathe but couldn't; I was back in Aleppo, gripped with the same fear as when we heard helicopters flying overhead, ready to drop barrel bombs.

The other kids dove toward us, and we huddled together. Mr. Fowler stood guard, shielding us with his arms.

I pinched the soft skin on my wrist, *snap out of it*. The pain refocused me and I exchanged a fearful look with Jordyn.

The chairwoman bellowed, "Mr. Sawyer, don't take another step. This behavior will not be tolerated!"

"Let go of me!" Mr. Sawyer yelled. "I have rights!"

I heard screams and confusion, but Mr. Fowler's voice cut through the chaos. "Kids, you can relax now. The security guard is escorting Mr. Sawyer from the building."

As many in the audience broke into applause and we climbed into our seats, the chairwoman smoothed down her jacket and took a deep breath. "Do I have a motion to uphold the superintendent's recommendation?" she asked.

The motion was made, seconded, and received a unanimous vote from the board members.

"Thank you all for attending," the chairwoman said. "That concludes our business for this evening. The meeting is adjourned."

"I can't believe Nick's dad went ballistic," muttered Lea as Daksha and Jordyn nodded in agreement.

"He had a right to voice his opinion," Mr. Fowler said, his face pale. "But he can't act the way he did and not expect there to be consequences."

"Man," grumbled Penny. "After all that drama we have to wait."

Ammar's fists were clenched, and Joel patted him on the back.

"This is not fair," mumbled Jordyn, leaning in toward me.

I nodded, stunned, as we huddled around Mr. Fowler.

Lea angrily tossed her head.

"I know you're all disappointed," Mr. Fowler said. "I am too, but regardless of what happens next, I'm proud of you guys. I know you'll grow up to be informed citizens, the kind our country desperately needs."

"What if they pass the buck . . . vote no?" I whispered.

"Then we'll keep believing that someday they'll vote yes," Mr. Fowler said. "Remember: 'The arc of the moral universe is long, but it bends toward justice.'"

CHAPTER THIRTY-SIX

❧ JORDYN ❧

Thursday, May 4, 2017

When I got to social studies class, Mr. Fowler was serving Krispy Kreme doughnuts, milk, and juice.

I grabbed a warm glazed doughnut and took a seat behind Noura. She turned and gave me a slightly dazed smile. "I have never had a Krispy Kreme doughnut before. I think I'm in love."

"But why are we celebrating?" I asked. "The board didn't even vote."

Noura shrugged. "I am not sure, but I'm always happy to eat doughnuts."

Mr. Fowler wiped his hands on a napkin and marched to the front of the room. His bushy eyebrows were practically jumping. "As we've previously discussed, the fight for justice is never really over, but last night you kids made me proud to be a teacher. It was a sight to behold—true civic engagement and participation in our political system! I brought in doughnuts to show my appreciation."

Bailey leaned toward me. "What happened?" she whispered.

Before I got the chance to answer her, Mr. Fowler cleared his throat. "Group discussions only, please. Last night I spoke at the school board meeting along with Noura, Joel, Daksha, Penny, Lea, and Jordyn. Would anybody be interested in filling the rest of the class in on what happened?"

I raised my hand so I could be the one to answer Bailey's question. "Mr. Fowler told the school board how we have kids from a lot of different religions in this class, and that the First Amendment protects all of us. Noura talked about setting up the prayer room, and then the rest of us shared our experiences using it, and why the room is important to us. We were a little nervous speaking into a microphone with so many adults there, but we still managed to give pretty good speeches."

"Indeed!" Mr. Fowler said. "I've never had a group of students address the school board before. It was one of the highlights of my teaching career so far." He snapped his fingers. "How about a reenactment? Would those of you who spoke last night be willing to read your speeches to the class?"

Noura shyly ducked her head, but Penny and Daksha were

already out of their seats and headed to the front of the room. The rest of us soon followed. Our speeches went even better than before. I spoke last, and for once it didn't feel like a shark was gnawing at my insides, only a small group of minnows. When I took my seat, Mr. Fowler and the other kids clapped for us. That's what Dr. Kelley would call real progress.

"Joel, I'm sorry about your mom," Bailey said. "I didn't know."

"Thank you," he said. "She's doing much better."

"Until we started practicing," Penny said, "I didn't realize Castro had banned Christmas. I'm not religious, but we still have a tree and presents. Who wouldn't like a tree and presents?"

"Castro," Lea said. "He wanted complete control."

"So, anyway, what did the school board decide?" Bailey asked.

"They didn't reach a decision," Mr. Fowler said. "They'll vote in a couple weeks, on May seventeenth."

Lea crossed her arms over her chest. "Yeah, that's the part that made me angry. The superintendent suggested the board wait and vote at the next meeting, so we have no idea whether we get to keep the prayer room or not."

"That's true," Mr. Fowler said. He walked over to the whiteboard and pointed to the first Supreme Court case:

Engel v. Vitale (1962). "That case was fifty-five years ago, and we're still debating prayer in public schools. You guys are part of history. Democracy in action!"

"I was impressed kids were allowed to speak and they took us seriously," Ammar said. "In Syria, and lots of other countries too, that would have been impossible. Freedom of speech is not allowed everywhere."

"Are you sure you couldn't say whatever you wanted to in Syria?" Nick asked, with a skeptical look on his face.

"I am positive," Ammar said. "Boys as young as twelve who wrote graffiti against the government were arrested and tortured. It led to our civil war."

Mr. Fowler thoughtfully nodded. "Because Noura and Ammar grew up in Syria, they bring a different perspective to free speech," he said. "Sometimes Americans take it for granted. Last night, we had the chance to make our voices heard. That's always worth celebrating."

When he put it that way, I didn't feel quite so glum, but still, two weeks was a long time to wait for an answer. "Any more doughnuts?" I asked.

"Help yourself," Mr. Fowler said with a grin. "I brought plenty."

CHAPTER THIRTY-SEVEN

❦ NOURA ❦

Wednesday, May 17, 2017

Raindrops beat against the windowpanes like a melodious drum as Mama hummed a Fairuz tune at the dining table, trying to figure out how the shiny new multiuse pressure cooker Baba had gotten for her worked. I sat on the sofa, hugging a soft cushion, appreciating the tantalizing smell of walnut *maamoul*, scented with cinnamon and rosewater, baking in the oven. I gazed out onto the balcony, searching for some feathered friends, hoping their antics would distract me for a while. But sadly, the wet weather had chased them away. With a sigh, I glanced at the clock on the wall for the hundredth time. The school board was voting today and Jordyn had access to the cable channel that would broadcast the proceedings. She had promised to call as soon as she found out the results. Filled with a nervous energy, I jumped off the sofa and began to pace.

"You know that won't make things go any faster," said

Ammar, frowning as he flipped through channels on the television, not really watching much of anything.

The volume was turned down low since both Baba and Ismail were asleep down the hall. Baba had started the night shift and usually came home around the time we were leaving for school.

"No, but it is better than sitting around," I said in a tight voice.

Ammar was irritated and cagey too. He'd finished his homework but hadn't been able to take the boys out for their usual soccer practice because of the rain.

"She'll call as soon as she finds out," said Ammar. "She promised."

"Children, come here," Mama said, giving us a knowing look. "I need help figuring out these instructions."

Ammar paused on a news channel and lumbered over to the table.

"The best way to keep your minds busy is to decipher a long and boring appliance manual," Mama said, and I couldn't help grinning. Her English was getting better with Mrs. Johnson's help, but the manual, with its minuscule print, was too much.

As Ammar examined the dozens of buttons on the pressure cooker and compared it to the manual, we heard the click of a door opening, followed by soft footsteps. Baba headed toward us in striped sleeping pants and a T-shirt, his hair sticking up along the sides.

"*Salaam Alaikum*, Baba, that's a cool new hairstyle," I teased.

Baba looked in the hall mirror and posed like he was a famous old-school Syrian singer. Hooded eyes, puffed-out chest, and pouty lips. We all laughed, the tension in the room easing.

"I'm famished," said Baba, taking a seat on the sofa.

"The stew is simmering," Mama said. "It won't be ready for another hour."

"How about a cheese sandwich?" I asked, wondering how many heavy suitcases he had carried last night. "I can make you one."

"That would be delicious," said Baba. "A cup of tea too, please."

I put on the kettle and opened the fridge to get the soft creamy cheese Baba loved. As I sliced the bread, Baba stretched out his legs and picked up the remote. He turned the volume up, and we heard an angry young man shouting. My eyes were riveted to a large group marching around a statue. They carried burning torches while chanting "White lives matter!" followed by "Build the wall!" Horrified, I couldn't look away.

The camera cut back to a newscaster sitting in a studio, her voice somber. "That was the scene a few nights ago from Lee Park in Charlottesville, Virginia. A group of white nationalists gathered to protest the city council's vote to remove the statue of Confederate general Robert E. Lee. General Lee is considered by many to be a symbol of the South's racist past, a man who fought to keep slavery during the Civil War. In the current political climate . . ."

"What are they saying?" Mama asked.

"It's nothing," said Baba, quickly switching off the television.

"Yusuf, tell me the truth," said Mama, placing her hands on her hips.

Ammar and I shared an anxious look. Mama had probably picked up enough to get an idea. But before she could say anything else, the sharp ring of the telephone echoed from the counter. Without thinking, I lunged for it before Ammar could. *It had to be her . . .*

"Hello," I said hopefully, forgetting about the news.

"Noura, is that you?" came a breathy voice. It was Jordyn. In the background, I could hear people talking, but it sounded like they were in a tunnel.

"Yes, it's me," I said, whirling back to face Mama, Baba, and Ammar. They looked at me expectantly.

"Noura, you won't believe it," Jordyn said.

"Believe what?" I switched over to the speakerphone and placed it on the dining room table. "What happened?"

"It was unbelievable," she practically shouted. "It was a unanimous vote."

My heart sank. "Everyone voted the same way?"

"Yes!" exclaimed Jordyn.

"Which way did they vote?" Ammar barked into the phone.

"Oh, sorry," said Jordyn. "They voted YES! We can keep the prayer room!"

I looked at Ammar, then at our parents, our expressions identical. Shock, then happiness, coupled with a hint of doubt.

"Are you sure?" I asked.

"Totally," said Jordyn. "I've texted practically everyone. We're all going to meet in the supply room tomorrow at lunch to fix it up. Lea's mom is getting the carpet dry-cleaned to get the glitter out. Daksha is making another COEXIST banner, and Penny promised to put up her trees again."

Strong emotions surged through me and for a moment I couldn't speak. Ammar gently took the phone from in front of me.

"Thank you, Jordyn," he said. "This is really, really great

news. We're looking forward to fixing up the room with everyone."

"Okay," Jordyn said. "I've got to go, I just got a text from Lea. I'll see you tomorrow."

After Ammar hung up, we all stood, looking at one another as Baba came to sit at the dining room table. "This is unbelievable," he said. "You two, along with your friends, made such an impressive case to the school board. I'm so proud of you."

"Thank you, Baba," I said with a grin. Though Ammar hadn't spoken, he'd helped me write my speech.

"And your teacher, that Mr. Fowler, should be commended on how he taught you to fight for your rights."

Mama had pulled the cookies out of the oven and was pouring tea. As we chatted, she came over with a tray and sat down with us. Her eyes solemn, she glanced at the television, then back at us. "Noura, Ammar," she said, her voice soft but serious. It was a tone that told us to pay attention.

"Yes, Mama," we replied practically in unison.

Baba reached for a *maamoul* and took a bite, his eyes somber.

"Like your father, I am extremely proud of you," she said, passing us hot glasses of tea. "You've come to a new country and worked hard to be good students, good citizens. And I wish more than anything that your baba and I could protect you. Create a sanctuary for you like the one for the beautiful roseate spoonbills you saw on the boat ride."

Mama's words washed over me and the euphoria of our victory began to fade. I took a sip of my tea, burning my tongue.

Mama continued. "Outside the protection of our home, a lot of terrible things are happening. We still don't know who set fire to the mosque. Or who vandalized the prayer room at school. Yet we have been blessed with many of these good wolves, as you call them—the Johnsons and their church, your teacher, Mr. Fowler, and all those who came to our mosque for the interfaith service. This is all wonderful and you should enjoy the blessings of each day."

Baba looked at Mama with admiration. "Of course, your mama is right. We have won the battle to save your prayer room, but there will be bigger challenges ahead."

Mama sighed in agreement and passed around the cookies. "But for now, enjoy your victory. Eat." She got up and went to the kitchen to stir the pot of stew. Baba headed to the bathroom to take a shower, and Ammar wandered off to his room.

I sat at the dining table, the warm *maamoul* resting on my palm as Mama began to sing. It was a song from one of the greatest Egyptian singers of all time, Umm Kulthum.

"Rise with faith, spirit, and conscience;
Step on all difficulties and move on.
Your country needs you;
It needs much effort.
Step on all difficulties and move on . . ."

I felt the warmth and love of my family settle into my bones, but the lyrics of the song dug into my heart. Tomorrow, Ammar and I would rise with faith, spirit, and conscience to fix the prayer room with our friends. But the day after . . . the day after, we would have to deal with hate. Hate that had led to the fire at our mosque and the vandalizing of our prayer room.

As Mama's beautiful voice settled over me, I could hear Baba in the shower, and knew that Ammar was hard at work on one of his models, while Ismail slept, awash in playful dreams. I took a bite of the still warm *maamoul* and swallowed the love Mama had poured into her cookies. As long as I had my friends and family around me, I knew I could deal with practically anything.

CHAPTER THIRTY-EIGHT

⇒ JORDYN ⇐

Wednesday, May 17, 2017

Tomorrow we would repair the prayer room. It seemed everyone had a unique contribution to make, except for me—Penny and her trees, Lea with the rug, Daksha and her COEXIST banner. I rubbed the flying fish on my necklace, remembering the peaceful look on Noura's face at Shell Key Preserve. I thought about how swimming and flying both represent freedom. I was inspired to write a poem for Noura and hang it on the prayer room wall.

FLYING OVER WATER

I'm a gliding fish,
And you are a bird.
We met flying over water.
When the storms came,
You taught me to breathe,
And I taught you to float.
I'm a gliding fish,
And you are a bird.
We met flying over water.
Worse storms may come,
But I will breathe,
And you will float.
I'm a gliding fish,
And you are a bird.
We met flying over water.

AUTHOR'S NOTE BY
SHANNON HITCHCOCK

Writing this book was a lot like putting together a jigsaw puzzle. I discovered the first piece by connecting with a high school friend on Facebook. Beth's daughter, Cheyenne, had recently converted to Islam, and I was intrigued. I decided to research Islam, but I wasn't entirely sure where the journey would take me.

As I corresponded with Beth and Cheyenne, they expressed frustration with how Christians view Islam. Though I prided myself on being open-minded, I held some of the same misconceptions. Cheyenne asked, "Have you ever met a refugee?" That question stayed with me as I researched, watched the news, and conducted interviews.

My minister, Vicki Walker, provided the next puzzle piece. While vacationing in Turkey, Vicki had met a Syrian woman and her young son. The boy had held a handwritten sign that read: WE ARE FROM SYRIA. CAN YOU HELP US? THANK YOU. Vicki had snapped their picture and displayed it in her office. It tugged at her heart—and mine.

Vicki introduced me to Janet Blair, the Community

Liaison for Refugee Services, Suncoast Region. Janet arranged for me to meet several Syrian girls. They told me of their favorite desserts, the music of Nancy Ajram, and shared the prejudice they face from wearing hijabs.

I discovered much of my plot through research. I was especially drawn to the resilience of Syrian teens Yusra Mardini, Mohammed Qutaish, and Muzoon Almellehan. I included them in this book to draw attention to their remarkable stories.

As I watched the documentary *8 Borders, 8 Days* and stared at the photo of Alan Kurdi lying on the beach, I knew water would play an important part in my story. I decided to make Jordyn a competitive swimmer, and Noura a girl whose best friend had drowned.

From Missy Franklin's autobiography, I learned how panic attacks affected her swimming and got the idea for Jordyn's anxiety disorder.

The mosque fire, Mayor Bob Buckhorn's response, the interfaith service, and Jewish people giving chai to repair the mosque were all inspired by actual events that occurred in Tampa in 2017.

When I turned a draft of this novel in to my editor, Andrea Pinkney, she thought it was missing something, but offered to read it again. While contemplating revisions, I discovered *Escape from Aleppo* by N. H. Senzai, and wondered if I was missing the most critical puzzle piece of all—a Muslim voice. I asked Ms. Senzai if she would be interested in telling Noura's half of the story. Not only was she interested, but Naheed fleshed out the Alwan family in a more authentic way than I could have accomplished on my own, and suggested adding the prayer room, which turned out to be a pivotal part of the plot. This story wouldn't be nearly as satisfying without the diverse details and characters that Naheed brought to it.

The final puzzle pieces fell into place as I read true accounts of fleeing Syria. For educators interested in learning more, I highly recommend *A Hope More Powerful Than the Sea: One Refugee's Incredible Story of Love, Loss, and Survival* by Melissa Fleming and *We Crossed a Bridge and It Trembled: Voices from Syria* by Wendy Pearlman.

AUTHOR'S NOTE BY
N. H. SENZAI

After writing *Escape from Aleppo*, a story about a girl fleeing the horrors of the Syrian civil war, I thought I was done covering this emotional and challenging topic. But then I received an intriguing offer from Shannon Hitchcock: Did I want to cowrite a novel about two girls, one American, and the other a Syrian refugee? As I read Shannon's initial draft, it struck a chord within me, so I said yes.

Shannon was gracious as I brought my ideas to the table. I proposed writing in alternating chapters, with each girl telling her own story, and incorporating important current events. As a Muslim American married to a professor of Middle East politics, I'd been watching the seismic shift in the American political and social landscape with growing concern. Since the 2016 election, all the "-isms" and "-phobias" had skyrocketed: xenophobia, Islamophobia, homophobia, racism, and antisemitism—challenging issues affecting communities, adults, and children.

Our story begins with Noura and her family landing in Tampa, Florida, on the day of the Muslim ban. They are welcomed by Jordyn's family and their church, mirroring my husband's experience when they arrived as refugees from Afghanistan in 1979, fleeing the Soviet Union invasion. I fleshed out Noura and her family's story. Once a successful hotelier in the old city of Aleppo, Noura's father had joined the White Helmets when Noura's brother was trapped under rubble after an air strike. Like thousands of others, they'd fled Aleppo for a refugee camp in Kilis, Turkey, where Noura is treated for PTSD.

While writing the novel, we woke up to the mosque shooting in New Zealand that left fifty-one worshippers dead. It shocked us how hate and ignorance led to the taking of innocent lives, and it became important to incorporate themes of understanding and tolerance. Another threat to humanity, one that contributed to the Syrian War, is climate change. My son's elementary school took part in an environmental beach cleanup and this became part of the plot. We also added an absurd law, recently passed in Florida, banning the ban of plastic straws.

It was because of another law in Frisco, Texas, attempting to ban a prayer room established by Muslim students, that I suggested we add a similar room to our story. The room served as a place for students of all backgrounds to come together to celebrate their religious/spiritual beliefs, assemble peaceably, and express free speech. When the room is shut down, the children petition to redress the decision, all rights afforded under the First Amendment.*

As Shannon and I were finishing the book, we were shocked to see that a top Trump immigration official, Ken Cuccinelli, had reworked Emma Lazarus's iconic poem from the Statue of Liberty, which plays a key role in our story. He declared that instead of taking in "tired, poor, huddled masses," we should only embrace immigrants who could "stand on their own two feet" and "not become a public charge," adding later that the poem referred only to "people coming from Europe."

Although outwardly different, both Noura and Jordyn struggle to find a sense of belonging and freedom. These themes manifested themselves using birds and fish and the concept of flying over water. Noura loves birds and Jordyn has an affinity with fish. A boat ride to Shell Key Preserve, a bird sanctuary near Tampa, serves as a voyage where the girls help each other overcome their fears and deepen their friendship.

---

* **First Amendment to the Constitution of the United States of America** *Congress shall make no law respecting an establishment of religion, or prohibiting the free exercise thereof; or abridging the freedom of speech, or of the press; or the right of the people peaceably to assemble, and to petition the Government for a redress of grievances.*

MOHAMMED QUTAISH

Mohammed Qutaish was ten years old when protests started in Syria. As his home city of Aleppo was ravaged by war, Mohammed began making a model to rebuild it. He and his dad gathered materials from street debris—paper, boxes, wood scraps, and cardboard—but there were no colored pencils or glue to be found in Aleppo. Those were brought in from Turkey. Mohammed worked for three years on his model, and hung a note above it that said, THEY DESTROY. WE REBUILD.

As he worked, Mohammed built not only structures that had been demolished but designed improvements for an Aleppo of the future: solar panels, rooftop pools, helipads, and gardens.

Mohammed's model was transported out of Syria and displayed at Mmuseumm in New York City. From there it moved to the Skirball Cultural Center in Los Angeles, and to the Victoria and Albert Museum in London. Articles and pictures of Mohammed's model have been featured in the *New York Times* and *Architectural Digest*.

When Mohammed grows up, he wants to be an architect and help rebuild Syria.

MUZOON ALMELLEHAN

Muzoon Almellehan is from Daraa, in southwest Syria. In 2013, fighting forced Muzoon's family to abandon their home. Muzoon left everything behind, except her books. The family escaped to a Jordanian refugee camp. They lived in camps for three years.

While at the Za'atari camp, Muzoon noticed that lots of girls were dropping out of school to get married. Because Muzoon's dad was a schoolteacher, she understood the value of an education. She began visiting her friends' parents and campaigning against child brides.

In 2014, Muzoon was excited to meet Malala Yousafzai, when Malala visited the Za'atari camp. The two became fast friends, and Muzoon has been called the Malala of Syria.

When Muzoon was seventeen, her family immigrated to England, where she continued her education. She found school much different than in Syria. Muzoon had to adjust to carrying her books around in a backpack, changing classrooms, and the strange food in the school cafeteria. The English her classmates spoke was different from textbook English. They spoke faster and with accents. There was much to learn, but Muzoon was up to the challenge.

Two years after moving to Newcastle, Muzoon was appointed a Goodwill Ambassador by UNICEF. She said in a PopSugar interview, "I feel lucky to go to school every day, but I cannot be completely happy until every child all over the world can have access to the same right."

When she completes her education, Muzoon hopes to become a journalist, and someday, to return to Syria.

YUSRA MARDINI

Yusra Mardini is from the Syrian city of Damascus. She represented Syria in the 2012 FINA World Swimming Championships.

During the civil war, Yusra's home was destroyed. She then fled Syria with her sister, Sarah. They boarded an overcrowded boat bound for the island of Lesbos. When the boat started to sink, Yusra, Sarah, and two others climbed into the water and swam for three hours. They pulled the boat to safety, saving the lives of twenty people.

The Mardini sisters then immigrated to Germany. There Yusra began training for the Olympics. She competed on the first ever refugee team in Rio de Janeiro. Yusra said, "The most important thing in my life is swimming. Then speaking and doing things to help refugees."

Today, Yusra is a Goodwill Ambassador for the United Nations High Commissioner for Refugees (UNHCR). She hopes to compete in the 2021 Tokyo Olympics.

ACKNOWLEDGMENTS

It required all hands on deck to make *Flying Over Water* a reality. We would especially like to acknowledge early readers Whitney Smitherman, Aimee Reed, Saba Taylor, Nancy Stewart, Lorin Oberweger, Hena Khan, Imtiaz Ghori, Razan Asbahi, and Erum Khan; Dr. Tori Kelley for lending her expertise to Jordyn's counseling sessions; Dr. Ahsan Sheikh, a child psychiatrist who provided insight into PTSD and trauma; Hickory High swim coach Cathy Hitchcock for sharing her knowledge of competitive swimming; the Reverend Vicki Walker, who connected us with Janet Blair, the Community Liaison for Refugee Services, Suncoast Region; Janet Blair for answering our questions about the resettlement process; and Rhonda Sibilia, former broadcast journalist and public education activist for her help with the school board meeting.

Flying Over Water landed at the perfect publishing house. Thanks to our editor, Andrea Pinkney, and the entire team at Scholastic for taking a chance on our collaboration.

And finally, our deepest gratitude to our agents, Deborah Warren and Michael Bourret, who made the initial contact between us and always believed this book was possible.

ABOUT THE AUTHORS

N. H. SENZAI is the award-winning author of *Escape from Aleppo*, *Ticket to India*, and *Saving Kabul Corner*. Her first novel for young readers, *Shooting Kabul*, was the winner of the 2010 Asian/Pacific American Award for Young Adult Literature, was an NPR Backseat Book Club pick, and appeared on numerous awards lists. She lives in the San Francisco Bay Area with her family. Visit her online at NHSenzai.com.

SHANNON HITCHCOCK is the author of *One True Way*, *Ruby Lee & Me*, and *The Ballad of Jessie Pearl*. Her books have been featured on many state awards lists and have received acclaimed reviews. Shannon divides her time between Florida and North Carolina. For more, visit her at her website at shannonhitchcock.com